PRAISE FOR MAILBOAT IV
THE SHIFT IN THE WIND

"Great summer read! (Delves) into the lives of Lake Geneva residents and the tangled web their lives create. These fictional characters seem so real, and the actual landmarks in Lake Geneva being the story to life!"

~ Mary-Jane Woodward, reader

"Once again, Danielle Lincoln Hanna's twisty mind took my expectations and turned them into a new configuration.... New windows opened into old relationships and left me wondering if anyone was truly who I thought they were."

~ Elaine Montgomery, reader

"I have never read anything that describes the look and feel of Geneva Lake as well as Danielle has done. Her ability to bring us into the heads and hearts of her characters makes me feel like I know them intimately."

~ Brenda Dahlfors, reader

"You absolutely have me hooked for life!"

~ Pat Perkins, reader

Danielle Lincoln Hanna

MAILBOAT

The Shift in the Wind

HHP

HEARTH & HOMICIDE PRESS, LLC
MISSOULA, MT
2021

Paperback: ISBN 978-1-7330813-9-9
Ebook: ISBN 978-1-7373962-0-8

JOIN THE CREW

———— ⚓ ————

Ahoy, Shipmate!

If you feel like you're perched on a lighthouse, scanning the horizon for Danielle Lincoln Hanna's next book—good news! You can subscribe to her email newsletter and read a regular ship's log of her writing progress. Better yet, dive deep into the life of the author, hear the scuttlebutt from her personal adventures, spy on her writing process, and catch a rare glimpse of dangerous sea monsters—better known as her pets, Fergus the cat and Angel the German Shepherd.

It's like a message in a bottle washed ashore. All you have to do is open it...

DanielleLincolnHanna.com/newsletter

LAST TIME
IN LAKE GENEVA

———— ⚓ ————

Officer Ryan Brandt responds to a 911 call at the Mailboat and finds Captain Tommy bleeding from a gunshot wound and his mail jumper Bailey crying over him. This is the first time she's shown emotion for anyone, and Ryan quickly realizes that Tommy alone holds the key to Bailey's heart, closed after years of abuse in foster care. If Tommy lives, maybe there's hope of saving Bailey, too.

Tommy is airlifted to Froedtert Hospital in Milwaukee and Ryan drives Bailey to see him. Bailey feels like she's intruding; she isn't as close to Tommy as the other people in the waiting room. Besides, everyone she cares about either leaves her or dies. The universe couldn't be any clearer that she doesn't belong. But Ryan seems determined that she and the captain ought to be together.

Detective Monica Steele is furious that Chief Wade Erickson thought the murders of the last members of the Markham Ring were solved and the violence was over. Now Wade's best friend is fighting for his life. Shaken, she almost accepts the temptation of comfort from Ryan, her ex. But he has no idea the devastation he caused when he cheated on her ten years ago. He never knew that Monica had finally gotten pregnant. In the aftermath of his betrayal, she kicked him out and had an abortion—without ever telling him.

After days of drifting in and out of consciousness, Tommy comes to and finds Bailey at his bedside. He has no memory of what happened and Bailey has to inform him. Realizing how close he came to death, Tommy finally screws up the nerve to tell Bailey the secret he alone knows: His fugitive son was her unknown father.

Bailey slips away to a hospital bathroom, where she comes unglued. The thing she's literally dreamed of is true: Tommy is her grandfather. Far from bringing her joy, it fills her with terror. In her experience, family are those people you never get to keep, and losing Tommy is her worst nightmare. Terrified, she cuts off her visits with Tommy, much to Ryan's dismay.

Meanwhile, Bailey's foster dad Bud Weber is pleased with his handiwork; he taught Tommy a swift lesson, and he's confident the captain won't dare report Bailey's mysterious bruises again. But Bud's boss, The Man Upstairs, is furious. By working his own side gig, Bud has risked ruining The Man's own murderous plan. The Man lets Bud know that his services are no longer needed. He's fired.

Jimmy Beacon, the young dishwasher at Bud's restaurant, finally finds his courage to express his feelings to Bailey—only to discover her holding hands with Noah Cadigan, the boy who coached him on how to approach a girl in the first place. He storms off in a rage. Jimmy's elderly friend Roland Markham tries to comfort him. But when conversation turns to Jimmy's younger sister Amelia, who was kidnapped, raped, and murdered, Jimmy's fury overflows. Roland points out that Jimmy might, in fact, be closer to the killer than he knows; it's said his boss, Bud Weber, has a taste for little girls. Jimmy searches Bud's office and finds the bow Amelia was wearing the day she was killed.

At his wit's end with both Bailey and Monica, Ryan talks with Bill Gallagher, the police chaplain and a foster father many times over. He advises Ryan to let Monica share her side of the story—when she's ready—and to love Bailey relentlessly to overcome her years of abuse. Considering his own unreliable track record, Ryan isn't convinced he could be the pillar of strength Monica and Bailey need.

Jimmy confronts Bud Weber with his evidence, as well as his means of revenge—a homemade bomb. They chase each other through the crowded tourist town with the cops on their heels. When Jimmy closes in and pulls the cord, Bill Gallagher runs from the crowd and throws himself over Jimmy and the bomb, absorbing the blast with his own body. When the dust settles, he and Jimmy are dead, as well as a Lake Geneva police officer. Bud gets away barely scathed.

While Monica and Ryan spring to bring order to the chaos, Monica's phone rings. A mysterious voice asks if she's figured out yet that everything's connected, from the murders of the members of the Markham Ring to this apparently unrelated bombing by a troubled youth. The voice claims to know the town's deepest secrets and how to exploit them—including Monica's. He implies that he knows about her aborted child.

When Monica demands to know his name, he replies: "I'm The Man Upstairs."

MAILBOAT

FRIDAY
JULY 11, 2014

CHAPTER ONE
RYAN

———— ✹ ————

Rain trickled along the black visor of my service hat in two glistening streams that pooled in the center, grew, thought about falling, then fell. One by one, the droplets struck my hands, clasped in front of me, and soaked into my white gloves. I ran my fingers along the brim, stopping the never-ending flow for a moment, and focused my attention on the young woman under the black canopy singing "Amazing Grace" in crystal tones while strumming a worn guitar.

The casket—closed—was white with gilded scrollwork. It dazzled even in the rain, as if the angels had ripped down the pearly gates and torn up the streets of gold to build it. As if nothing less would do for their beloved, fallen saint. Bill Gallagher. Our chaplain. The man who had saved hundreds of lives by throwing himself over a boy and his bomb. I'd never be able to erase the image of carnage. I still couldn't believe what Bill had done. In the microcosm of time between his spotting the bomber and his flinging himself over the boy, he'd made up his mind. Thrown aside life and everything it had to offer. Sacrificed himself for his town and the people he loved.

I hoped the angels had lined his casket with their own feathers to cradle his broken body. I hoped they greeted him with harps and a crown of glory.

He deserved it.

I flicked my head to shake off another droplet and turned my eyes to Bill's family, standing under the black canopy. His wife Peggy. His three children by birth. His four children by adoption. The seven of them grown with partners and kids of their own, an army of grandchildren.

Two kids stood center front, Peggy's hands on their shoulders. A boy and a girl, maybe six or seven. Their position with the family was uncemented. They were Bill and Peggy's last two foster children. With the tragedy that had struck her life, Peggy could have easily picked up the phone and asked social services to re-home them. No sooner asked than done, the kids would have been out of her house within twenty-four hours. To re-home them so quickly, the kids probably would have been split up. Given the unpredictable path of foster care, they might never have seen each other again.

But clearly Peggy hadn't called. There they stood with the family as if they were blood-born and not someone else's forgotten children. Bill wouldn't have had it any other way. Once a child entered under his roof, that child was forever a Gallagher, in spirit if not in name.

The young woman with the guitar strummed the final chord. Her voice trailed to silence. Rain thrummed on the canopy and the coffin. Chief Wade Erickson stepped up to a microphone and raised it several inches to match his height. His navy blue uniform sported five gold stars, signifying him as the highest ranking official in the Lake Geneva Police Department. His eyes traversed the crowd—friends and family in black, police officers in navy blue.

"We are gathered here to lay to rest our brother, Bill Gallagher, a beloved pastor, chaplain, friend..." His eyes traveled to the family. "...father, grandfather, and husband."

3

Peggy smiled with soulful gratitude and hugged the children closer.

Wade turned again to the crowd, his jaw working emptily for a moment. "But beyond that, Bill was... the bravest man I have ever had the honor of knowing." His eyes went hollow, haunted. As if the shock of Bill's sacrifice hit him as hard as it did all of us. Wade soldiered past the look of emptiness, found his words again. "He was a man so full of love for his fellow creatures, whoever they may be, that he willingly laid down his life for them, with no regard for his own."

The chief's open vulnerability triggered my own. A lump rose in my throat, choking off my windpipe. My memory flashed back to one of my last conversations with Bill. *Relentless love.* That's what we'd talked about, this insane concept he'd introduced me to. A love so resolute, nothing could force it to back down. Not fear, not rejection, not even a boy with a bomb.

"Am I capable of relentless love?" I'd asked that night.

"We all are," Bill had replied. *"If we want to be."*

And the very next day, I'd gone and decided I wasn't. Like a coward, I'd started filling out apps for other departments. Other jobs I could work when my temp patrolman's job in Lake Geneva ended. Places far away from Bailey Johnson, the foster girl I cared about beyond explanation. From Monica Steele, my ex, whom I still loved with all my heart.

But not with relentless love.

That had been before the bomb. Before the fear of losing Bailey and Monica had become horrifyingly real. Bill's selfless act of love for complete strangers shamed me from beyond the grave. Was I too weak and afraid to love Bailey and Monica as relentlessly as he had loved this town?

Bill had also challenged me to quit dwelling on myself, on my lead-weighted feelings of worthlessness and shame.

In a nutshell, he told me to focus on getting shit done. Being there for Bailey despite my fears and probable incompetence. Figuring out what it really was Monica needed, then either providing it for her or getting the hell out of her way so she could get it done herself.

I fixed my eyes on the casket and drew a shaky breath. Bill had had a way of shedding a spotlight on things that made them so simple, the path laser clear. Was there any hope I could hang onto that light, even without him around to make sure the battery was fully charged?

I heard his voice in my head. *Yes, you can, Ryan. If you want to.*

"Let's pray," Wade Erickson said. "Heavenly Father..."

I tipped my chin toward my clasped hands—but not before glancing down the military-straight row of my brothers and sisters in blue. Monica Steele stood at the far end next to her partner, Detective Sergeant Stan Lehman. She looked amazing in her tailored, navy blue dress uniform, her gold insignia and badge shining, her glossy mahogany hair twisted in a tight bun at the base of her neck, below her service cap. She was a solid wall of poise and determination—but also feminine elegance—a lethal combination of elements a man would be crazy to mess with.

That's what I'd always loved about her. Her strength. Her will. This woman could take care of herself. And yet, once upon a time, she had permitted me into her life. To love her. To stand beside her. To see her vulnerable side. To be her husband. Her lover. She set me on fire like no one else ever had or ever would.

"...in Jesus' name," Wade concluded, "Amen." And I realized I'd forgotten to pray to anyone but the goddess at the end of the row.

"Amen," the crowd muttered.

"Amen," I joined in.

5

Feet stirred, but for a moment, no one spoke, no one moved. Finally, Peggy Gallagher stepped toward the casket. Laid a single red rose on the lid. Laid her arm across her entombed husband. Whispered. Wept. Then walked away.

Her children and grandchildren were next, laying their roses on top of Peggy's until they'd built a pyramid of red and green. Brothers and sisters hugged each other. Cried.

Last of all, Bill's final two foster children stepped forward. With down-turned faces, they hesitated. But Peggy smiled and encouraged them forward. Standing on tiptoe, the boy nestled something orange, red, and fuzzy amidst the flowers. When he stepped away, I saw what it was. The knitted lion hat Bill had worn while playing with the children. Perhaps the one item these kids most associated with him. With his love. His relentless love.

Don't let me down, Ryan, his voice whispered through my head again. *You can do this.*

As the crowd began to break up, rearrange itself, converse in hushed tones, I looked toward Monica. Lehman had left. She was talking with Steph Buchanan, one of the telecommunicators. Without me really telling them to, my feet carried me toward Monica—as if they'd known all along what to do and had just been waiting for my head and my fears to get out of the way.

CHAPTER TWO
MONICA

He was looking at me. Ryan. Just standing in the rain, staring like a sad puppy. I took a deep, shaky breath and tried to focus my attention on my conversation with Steph. If Ryan had noticed me tremble, hopefully he would attribute it to the funerals—Bill's today, Mike Schultz's yesterday. Losing both our chaplain and a fellow officer, and burying them one after the other, had left me shattered. But no one needed to know that.

I'd barely spoken to Ryan since the day the bomb went off downtown. He'd thrown himself on top of me to protect me from the shrapnel. And now I could barely look at him, much less speak to him. His nearness sent shivers through my body like it used to lifetimes ago, and I couldn't begin to explain it. He still loved me. It was obvious in his every move, his every look.

The terrifying question was... what if I still loved him?

By the time I saw him coming towards me, the drowned puppy now hopeful, it was too late to run. Oh, God, why? My mind scrambled to maintain the threads of my conversation with Steph. If I looked occupied, if Ryan could feel the ice rolling off my shoulders, maybe he would leave me alone.

But just as I thought of something to add to the conversation, Steph squeezed my hand. "I'm going to talk to Angie."

"Yeah, sure." My mouth betrayed me with a smile. What I really wanted to say was, *No, Steph, cover my six here.* Didn't she see Ryan coming? But maybe she did, and maybe that was why she was walking away—to give us space to be alone.

Great.

Ryan cocked his head, eyes searching for clues as to my demeanor today. He approached me cautiously as he always did. But his spine remained straight. That's just what a dress uniform does to your psyche; it's impossible to slouch, to disrespect yourself or this sign of your office. It brings out the best in you.

And it brought out the best in Ryan. The straight lines of his jacket underscored his calm, his command. Meanwhile, his compassion shone out from a pair of coffee-brown eyes under his rain-speckled visor. His well-toned biceps filled out his sleeves. He was gorgeous. I'd always been a sucker for a guy in uniform.

No, that wasn't true. I'd always been a sucker for Ryan in uniform. There had never been any other guy. Not even after I dumped him.

He stopped in front of me. Dipped his head and scratched the back of his neck. "A bunch of us are going to Foley's," he said. It was a bar on the north side of the lake. "You know. After the reception."

No surprise. As cops, we swallowed as much heartache as we did coffee and liked to wash them both down with something stronger at the end of the day. Especially a day like this.

Ryan glanced in different directions and then at me. "You, ah... you want to come?"

I furrowed my brow. He was... inviting me to drinks? In what way? Was I just joining the group? Or was I *going out* with him?

"Uh..." I hesitated.

He lifted a palm. "You know, whatever you want to do."

His rush to offer an escape implied he'd hoped for the latter—that I would go out with him. My stomach twisted into knots. The same place it always did, right beneath my solar plexus. The empty place. The place where I'd briefly carried our child. Ryan still knew nothing. Never had a chance to. I'd seen him with another woman, then ended the pregnancy without telling him a word. Even though I tried to convince myself that I was okay with my decision, my psyche was a wreck.

I forced sounds through my lips. "I was just going to go back to the office."

He huffed a laugh through his nose. "Oh. Of course." The smile on his mouth implied humor, fondness, and familiarity.

He knew I didn't have a life away from my desk in the detective bureau—and apparently he found that endearing. Of course, he and I had always lived life in the fast lane. He understood my need to be busy. Especially now. Three weeks ago, we had found a man from California tied to the end of a pier on the lake. His ID said his name was Will Read. Our records knew him better as Fritz Geissler, the boy who had grown up in Lake Geneva, the young man who had made millions breaking into banks as part of a ring, the fugitive we'd been seeking for seventeen years.

Things had only gotten worse when his last living partner in crime, Jason Thomlin, had turned up dead as well. Then Jason's father Tommy had been shot. Then a bomb had gone off in the middle of downtown.

And then someone we still hadn't identified had called my personal cell phone. Claimed to be the one behind it all.

Called himself The Man Upstairs. And he suggested he knew about my unborn child.

I really didn't have time for things like Foley's.

"You won't take one night off?" Ryan asked with a hopeful smile I remembered well. "For Bill? For Mike?"

I glanced away over the gathering of mourners. "I'll see how I feel. After the reception." At the moment, I felt sick to my stomach. Thinking about The Man Upstairs did that to me. So did thinking about the secret I was hiding from Ryan.

He nodded. "Fair enough. Need a ride back to the church?"

"No." I'd brought my own car.

"Okay." He toed the grass but made no move to leave. For several seconds, we both stood awkwardly. He finally cleared his throat and gestured toward the black canopy and the line of people waiting to extend their condolences to the family. "I'm gonna give my regrets to Peggy."

I nodded. Good. I needed him to go. Now. But he lingered as if hopeful I'd come with him. When I didn't, he nodded, then strode away through the sprinkling rain. The water had darkened the shoulders of his jacket and the top of his hat.

He was gone. Finally. Great. I supposed I should go mingle, if nothing else than to confirm my verbal cues with a physical one and show Ryan I wasn't even thinking about him anymore. But I hated the thought of making small talk. There was no one here I wanted to spend time with.

Except Ryan.

Eventually, I forced myself to join my partners from the detective bureau, Stan Lehman and Mark Neumiller. We talked about the rain, and when was the last time any of the patrol units had a wax? Maybe they were due. But my eyes kept drifting to Ryan.

When he finally got to the head of the line under the canopy, he gave Peggy Gallagher a hug. She wrapped him in a tight embrace, a ferocious mama bear whose felt duty was to comfort all those around her. A woman who wouldn't shed her own tears until she was home, in the solitude of the room she'd shared with the love of her life. And then the tears would flow. That was her nature.

Two young children stood by her side. Grandkids, maybe. Or fosters, though it stretched my imagination to think the Gallaghers were still taking in children after so many years. To my surprise, Ryan got down on his knee, looked the kids in the eyes, and said something I couldn't hear. But the kids dropped their gazes to the ground. Nodded. Seemed to appreciate whatever it was he'd said, in their small, innocent minds.

As if to move away from feelings she didn't know what to do with, the little girl looked up with a smile and offered Ryan the leaf she'd been twirling in her hand. Ryan accepted it, then cupped the back of her head and planted a kiss on her forehead.

The sight twisted a knife in my soul. I'd always joked Ryan would make a terrible dad, back in the days when we were trying—and failing—to have a baby. I'd been teasing him, but it had probably been true. Ryan had still been a footloose, carefree soul, pulling pranks at work and enjoying the freedom we still had as a childless couple. Starting a family had been my idea, not his. In hindsight, I'd grabbed his wrist and yanked him all the way down that road, barely asking him what he thought, simply assuming he wanted a family as much as I did. Maybe that was why he'd made himself an out. Maybe that was why he'd slipped home another woman when he thought I was away and blown up every bridge between us.

But we'd been apart ten years, and now here he was, listening to a pair of children ramble on, accepting priceless little tokens that were going to shrivel up later that afternoon. Looking as if he would have been so goddamn natural at the job of parenting. There was Bailey Johnson for proof, too. Ryan was married to the mission of getting her out of her abusive foster home. When she was around, wings practically sprouted from his back and wrapped around her like feathered shields.

What had happened to the Ryan I knew? It was as if he'd shed everything I hated, kept everything I loved, and added a few things I never dreamed of. The new Ryan was irresistible. He was perfect. His soul called to my soul, and my soul screamed to take him back.

But our relationship had been built on honesty. There was no way it could survive after everything we'd done to each other. How could he cheat on me? How could I have made this decision about our baby without so much as telling him? Without including him? My reasons at the time had been bulletproof. But now…

Nausea wrenched my stomach again and tears flooded my eyes. Neumiller and Lehman were comparing the virtues of various brands of car wax, barely noticing me anymore.

"I'll see you at the reception," I blurted and turned away. I made for the cars parked by the road.

They stopped talking and watched after me but didn't stop me. I just kept going, shoulders square, trying to hold it in as long as possible. They would think I was crying for Bill or Schultz or both, and that was fine.

But I wasn't. I was crying for the life Ryan and I used to have together. The new stage in life we'd almost had together. The life we hadn't actually been ready for.

Finding my own car, I planted one hand on the hood and fisted the other one to my mouth, trying to push back all the years of second-guessing and regrets. Trying to accept the impossibility of ever getting together with Ryan again.

Because now, ten years later, he would be the best dad ever. And I couldn't imagine how to tell him he would have had a child of his own. There was no way he'd understand why I'd made my decision, without a single word to him. He'd be devastated. He'd never speak to me again.

And I couldn't blame him.

CHAPTER THREE
ANGELICA

—————— ⚙ ——————

To cross the Wisconsin border in the middle of a rain shower felt appropriate. Angelica Read held the steering wheel in both hands, grounding herself with the feel of firm leather beneath her sweating palms, and followed the prompts from the screen on the dash. She'd told the map to take her to Lake Geneva without being more specific. There was no friend she'd come to visit. No hotel she wanted to check into. No restaurant to try. No attraction to take in.

She just wanted to find the place, hear the map tell her, "You have arrived," and breathe. Then she'd drive aimlessly for as long as she needed. Explore the streets. The neighborhoods. The outskirts. Wrap her mind around the idea that this place was in fact real.

This place where her husband, Will Read, had grown up. Where, three weeks ago, he had been murdered. Drowned. Left tied to a pier post somewhere in a lake she'd never heard of before. Because he had never told her.

While the rain was perfectly on cue, the corn was a surprise. There was just so much of it. And not a billboard in sight. No flashy signs advertising the numerous delights to be had if you only pulled off the highway for a moment.

14

For a popular Chicago tourist destination, this town gave no hint it existed, beyond a few unassuming green signs along the road. Lake Geneva, twenty miles. Lake Geneva, ten miles...

As the distance shrank, her soul twisted into ever tighter knots. Should she be here? Should she be asking questions about her husband's past? Was it better to live with a beautiful lie—a shrine to a beautiful nothing—or to know the ugly truth?

Her hands tightened on the wheel as her resolution grew firm. Truth. It was always better to know the truth. That was what she and Will had always valued togeth—

The tears wrenched free. In a moment, she could barely see the road. She twisted her head, fighting the pain. Truth? What was truth anymore? How could she say she valued truth when her entire marriage had been a falsehood? A flimsy stage prop? A cheap roadside attraction? Light and mirrors and illusions? *A lie?*

But still, ten thousand questions screamed for answers. The desire to feel something firm under her feet demanded her attention. All of it. She could no longer sit at home in LA pretending to grieve like a normal widow. She hadn't merely lost a husband. She had lost every precious moment with a man she only *thought* she knew. A man who had played her, and played her well.

She would seek the truth, even if the word itself was now tainted in her mind.

She turned onto another country highway, one of a million that seemed to spiderweb northern Illinois and southern Wisconsin. An iron fence appeared on her right, and instead of green stalks, stone monoliths cropped up from the ground. There was a black canopy. A crowd. A white casket on a scaffold. A funeral. Like the rain, this, too, felt appropriate.

Filled with morbid curiosity, she scanned the crowd. A military funeral? Half the people were dressed in uniform. But then she saw the dozens of police cars.

Returning her eyes to the road, she pressed her lips together and remembered to breathe. She was naturalized now. Her parents were, too, and her aunt and uncle and cousins. It had taken twenty years, but it had happened. For all of them. Still, she often had to remind herself she was no longer an undocumented immigrant. There was nothing to fear.

But when she had married Will, and especially when the boys had been born, she would sometimes lie awake at night. What if they arrested her? What if they sent her back to a country she barely knew anymore? What if she never saw her boys again? What if she lost everything they had gained together?

Will's job as a bank executive had allowed them every luxury they wanted. He'd encouraged her to follow her passion of becoming a realtor. She loved beautiful homes. They'd had their two sons. Lived in a house in Malibu with a view of the ocean. They'd created a life together beyond her wildest dreams. And in the back of her mind, she feared losing it all because she didn't have paperwork. No one could hand her a form to fill without her heart rate going up. What if it asked...?

On nights when the fears were too real, she would cling to Will and cry into his shoulder. Even in his sleep, he would wrap an arm around her. Mutter that everything would be okay. That he loved her. And somehow, she had believed that love as real as theirs was equal to anything the world could throw at them. It was all that got her through.

But when it turned out a man had told you nothing about himself—nothing that was true—could such a love have been real at all?

Three weeks ago, Will had flown to a conference in Las Vegas. That was what he told her. Then he quit calling and texting. Then there had been a ring at her bell. Two police officers. They told her that her husband was dead. Murdered. He had never been in Vegas. He was killed in a small town in Wisconsin. They told her they had no answers. They left her blank. Hanging. Confused. Disoriented. She told herself they had identified the wrong person. She didn't know why Will didn't call, but they *had* to have the wrong person. He'd never been to Wisconsin in his life.

Then a detective from Lake Geneva, a woman named Monica Steele, had flown all the way to Los Angeles to tell her that her husband had been a fugitive. A bank burglar. A member of an infamous ring. A man named Fritz Geissler, not Will Read. And did Angelica know where his accomplice was?

Angelica flared her nostrils and wrung the steering wheel. No. No, she did not know where his "accomplice" was. What was the woman talking about? This was madness.

But the days had rolled on and Will had not come home. The papers and news stations reported that a long-lost member of the "infamous" Markham Ring was dead. Then they sent his body. They flew it home. They asked her to identify him. The police showed her a picture of Will's face. His face after death. Calm. Composed. Lifeless.

She broke in two.

It was true, then. Will was gone.

They had a funeral. It was small. Few friends showed up. No one knew what to say. Her family wept. Brought her food. Tried to comfort her.

There was no comfort for this.

She'd sent her boys to her parents' and come to Lake Geneva for answers. Answers about the man she'd loved.

17

The man she'd devoted ten years of her life to. The man she'd never actually known.

How could he lie to her like this? How could he betray her? He was her heart. Her everything.

It turned out, she'd never even known his real name.

CHAPTER FOUR
RYAN

I paused outside the door to the chief's office, cupped my hand to my mouth, and breathed. Yep. I smelled like beer. Also, I'd changed out of my uniform ages ago and was now dressed in ratty jeans and a tee shirt. Well, Wade had known I was going to Foley's. If he'd wanted me well-dressed and sober, he should have texted me earlier in the evening.

I knocked on his door.

"Come in."

I entered. He sat at his desk, leaning his jaw on his fist. He was still wearing his dress uniform from the funeral, but he'd pulled off his tie and loosened his collar. The windows behind his desk were black, the blinds forgotten open. The room was softly lit by the floor lamp behind his desk, easier to reach from his chair than the light switch by the door. Put together, the evidence suggested he'd been sitting here for hours.

"Burning the midnight oil, sir?" I asked, closing the door behind me.

He shuffled the stack of papers he'd been looking at. "No shortage of oil to burn."

19

"True," I agreed. "How's the task force getting along?" After three homicides, a shooting, and a bombing, all tied to a cold case with no end of leads to follow, Monica and her partners in the detective bureau had simply run out of manpower and daylight hours. They'd reached out to both neighboring and overarching departments, asking for aid, and those departments had swooped in to help the way you'd rush to a kid getting his ass pounded on the playground. That's about how our department felt. And that's about how the other departments felt, watching us.

"They're keeping plenty busy," Wade said. "But that's not what I called you in to talk about." With his pen, he pointed to a chair in front of his desk. "Have a seat."

I sat, half wondering if I'd done something wrong. Getting called into the chief's office was about as tense as being called into the principal's office.

Wade rotated his stack of paperwork so it faced me. The one on top said "W2."

"Fifty-one thousand a year," Wade said. "All the usual benefits and pension. And you can park the ten-speed. We'll get you a patrol car." He threw the pen down on top and leaned back in his chair.

I glanced between the paperwork and Wade. He was offering me a year-round job. He wanted me off the summer reserves. Off bike patrol. And I knew why. He was short an officer. Mike Schultz was dead.

The fan inside Wade's computer hummed to life, only emphasizing the silence. A few months ago, when I'd applied for a job in my hometown, I would have been thrilled to get a year-round. That was before I'd known Monica was working at our home department again, too. I'd known better than to kick the broken bee's nest of our relationship. But for some reason, Wade had never thought to warn me that I'd be working with my ex again when he hired me on.

I coughed into my fist. Shifted in my seat. "You, ah... You want me to stay?"

Wade nodded.

"Permanently?"

"Yeah."

"You'll lose Monica." I'd heard the rumors. She'd threatened to resign if I didn't leave by the end of the summer like I was supposed to.

Wade shook his head. "Monica's not going anywhere."

I raised an eyebrow. "What makes you so sure?"

"She'll never leave you."

Wade's words socked me like a brick to the chest, not least because he well knew I was the one who had left her ten years ago. Well, I had cheated on her, and she'd kicked me out. Same difference. I gaped at the chief, waiting for my lungs to function again. He simply punched me again.

"She's in love with you. Always has been, always will be."

I laughed, finally finding the air for such a thing. "Is that why she invites me to go down-range any time she's practicing?" In her eyes, I made a more appropriate shooting target than the paper posters.

Wade looked me pointedly in the eye. "That's why she's never dated anyone else."

That stopped me. He was right. In the ten years we'd been apart, I'd gone out with whole carousels of women. But Monica? I'd never so much as heard that she'd gone for drinks with anyone. Taken in a movie. So far as I knew, she'd never even let someone jog with her on her morning runs. The vast, sheer loneliness of the past decade of her life slammed into me full force.

Wade drummed a finger on his desk. "Ryan, I knew the day I accepted your app for bike patrol that there were going to be fireworks. I also knew it would be nothing but a show. Because that woman has loved you and no one else since high school." He twisted his head and lifted his hands.

"She was going to demand her pound of flesh, absolutely. But that's only because she could never dream of being with anyone else."

And I screwed it up, I added silently. I toyed with a rip at the knee of my jeans. "I just thought you'd forgotten we had a history." I shrugged. "I mean, either that or you enjoy watching gladiatorial combat."

Wade chuckled. "I didn't get to be chief of police by not knowing my officers." He nodded his chin at the pen and the sheet of paper. "Go on. Sign it."

I hesitated, then tapped the page, eying Wade dubiously. "You're telling me that if I sign this, Monica won't pack up her desk tomorrow?"

Wade steepled his fingers and shook his head. "Not tomorrow or any other day. Especially not with a case like this on her hands."

He had a good point. Monica would never abandon her hometown right when it needed her.

I drew a deep breath. So this was it, then. The moment when I decided once and for all whether I was staying or going. If I was the drifter or the dreamer. If I was ready to take up the challenge of relentless love. For Monica. For Bailey. And let's face it—for me. For my own dreams. For my own future. For possibilities I could barely glimpse, even if I couldn't quite believe in them yet.

I swallowed down one last gulp of terrified insecurity. Then I grabbed the pen and firmly scrawled my name.

Wade smiled. "Welcome home, Ryan.

SATURDAY
JULY 12, 2014

CHAPTER FIVE
TOMMY

———— ✹ ————

Wade had me cushioned in so many pillows and blankets, I'd hardly need the airbags if they went off. He kept glancing between the road and me as if he were taking a newborn home from the hospital. Well then, why didn't he just put me in a car seat?

Worried as he was about *my* health, he looked positively terrible, like he hadn't slept in a week. He'd been at a funeral last night and another one the day before that. I wasn't sure he had any business picking me up from the hospital today. He'd lost an officer, Mike Schultz. Bill Gallagher, the chaplain, had died, too. Maybe that was why Wade was worried about me. There'd been a lot of death lately.

A lot of death. And somehow, I was still alive. I wasn't sure why I'd been the lucky one. If this was luck.

"You comfortable, Tommy?" Wade asked for the third time.

I sighed and turned to gaze at the grass and the trees flying past the passenger-side window. We'd barely gotten on the interstate ten minutes ago.

"I'm fine," I grumbled. "Quit treating me like I'm made of glass." I didn't tell him the half-healed bullet wound in my side ached with every vibration of the car.

Wade narrowed his eyes at me, upset that I'd taken offense to his concern. "You're a seventy-five-year-old man who took a bullet to the gut. I'm not even sure how you're alive right now."

Because I need to be, the answer flashed through my head. And maybe it was true. My son Jason was dead. I'd buried him alone, then waffled on whether or not to tell my mail jumper, Bailey, that she was my granddaughter—a fact I had only just learned. And then some renegade had pulled a gun on me. The reason was as blank to me as any memory of his face. I'd almost died before I had the chance to tell Bailey the truth. I'd dragged my carcass through drifting consciousness and crazy dreams for no other reason than that I *needed* to tell her. I'd never had the right to keep the truth from her.

I pictured vividly the day I'd finally woken up in the hospital after a thousand crazy dreams, fantasy and horror mixed with reality. And then the light was finally real, and there was Bailey sitting in a chair beside my bed. She smiled, as thrilled as the day she'd become a mail jumper. She smiled as if she were happy to see me. As if she were relieved. And then I finally—*finally*—told her the secret only I knew.

And I hadn't seen or heard from her since.

Not one word.

I still had no idea what she thought of having me as a grandfather. Maybe she recognized a flunky when she saw one. I hadn't done that great with her dad...

Wade broke into my thoughts. "Lindsey and Jon wanted to be at the house to greet you, but I told them we should wait. The kids can be pretty active, and I figured the drive might wear you out."

"Hm," was all I said. If I had my way, Wade would drop me off at my own house instead of holding me captive at his place for the foreseeable future. But the doctor had backed him one hundred percent, and not just so Nancy and Wade could assist with my recovery. Whoever had put a bullet in me, he was still on the loose. My own home was the last place I should be. The fact I was going to Wade's house instead was known to only a select few, and I was under strict orders not to share that info.

I struggled to admit it was better this way.

"The grill-off is next Sunday," he rambled on. "You'll see everyone then. I have to defend my title against Jon. Lindsey had no business marrying a man who can grill a tenderloin as good as he can. The competition's stiff, but I still have the best steak for two years running. Oh, and the kids are at summer camp this week. Brace yourself; you'll be required to be amazed at a literal mountain of badges and crafts, all at the same time."

I sighed, anger simmering. Above all, this was why I didn't want to stay at Wade's. I didn't need to be constantly reminded that his life had turned out better than mine. That he still had a wife and children. That his son had a sparkling career in the Air Force. That his daughter was a beloved teacher and was happily married to a hard-working welder. That Wade had a pair of beautiful, vivacious grandchildren and a third on the way. That they were all happy and healthy.

My wife was dead. My son was a fugitive, and he had been murdered. His girlfriend, whom I thankfully never met, had been a drug addict who died of an overdose. And my granddaughter—the one I didn't even know I had until now—was stuck in foster care with a man who sent her to work with bruises on her face and arms.

I closed my eyes. What had she said when I told her? What did she think? Why couldn't I remember her reaction? I'd spent my remaining weeks in the hospital

26

wracking my brain for the memory, but it was gone. My mind had chosen random information to delete. Like anything that could help Wade identify the person who had shot me.

Maybe Bailey hadn't answered at all. Or maybe I already had her reply: Three weeks of silence. Complete and total silence.

I leaned deeper into Wade's pillows and sighed, but shallowly so as not to trigger the pain in my side. The fact that Bailey had a grandfather didn't necessarily mean she needed one.

It didn't mean she even wanted one.

CHAPTER SIX
BAILEY

———————— ⚓ ————————

Standing at the counter at the front of the Mailboat, I prepped the mail for the day's run. I curled a newspaper around a stack of mail, then snapped a rubber band around the whole thing, securing it for the crazy thing that was Lake Geneva mail delivery—jumping from a moving boat to put the mail in the boxes on the piers.

That's when I saw that Brian, our stand-in captain, had misspelled the name written on the top corner of the newspaper. It was supposed to be *Olsen,* not *Olson.* Tommy never would have written a name wrong. I mean, he'd been delivering the Olsens' mail for, like, half a century.

But everything at the Mailboat was different now. We'd forget to stock the Doritos before heading out on the cruise, and of course there would be at least five tourists who really wanted a bag of Doritos. Or a cover would turn up dogeared on a magazine. Or the address would be smeared on an envelope because our hands were wet. We straight-up forgot to deliver to a house once. And my inner thighs were always sore, strained from jumping further than I was used to. Brian was afraid of getting too close to the wooden piers and knocking them down. I guess three weeks of driving the Mailboat didn't give you as much finesse as fifty.

Everything was a mess, barely bobbing along. And it was better this way. It would actually just be better if Tommy never came back. My brain still felt like it was exploding after what he'd told me.

That he was my grandpa.

I'd had a long time to think about it now. And crazy as it sounded, I didn't want him to be. I know, I know. His being my grandpa was *literally* the thing I used to daydream about. Thing is, dreams are great and all, but mostly because they aren't real. In my dreams, Tommy would love me, and we'd be super happy together, and we'd spend summer *and* winter together, and he would never, ever abandon me, like everyone else in my life literally. Foster care just sucks.

But now that he was really, truly, actually my grandpa... Something felt weird about it. Rotten. Like a peach that looks great on the outside but is all black and moldy on the inside, and the pit is just a fuzzy black ball of death. Something would happen to ruin everything. And I didn't want to be around when it did.

I looked up through the front window and my eyes crossed, blurring the bow of the boat and the beach and the Riviera Ballroom. For a moment, I kind of wasn't on the Mailboat anymore. I was crouched on the pavement in the middle of a blackened street and bullets were zinging over my head. And a perfect stranger—a man who had tipped me a hundred dollars at my other job as a waitress—was using his last breaths on this earth to fire back, trying to save my life.

I kind of wish he'd used his last breath to tell me he was my dad instead, and then I could have just died amazed and happy. He would have been everything I'd hoped and dreamed of. A superhero.

Instead, he died without telling me a thing. He left that job to Tommy, who also informed me that my dad had been a bank burglar, a cop killer, and a fugitive. Had he even known I existed before that night? Apparently not.

And with that information, I was now just as confused about my dad as I was about Tommy. How was I supposed to feel about either of them anymore? How come my life couldn't just turn out the way I wanted?

The sound of gulls screeching as they found something interesting on the beach helped bring me back. Uncrossing my eyes, I dropped my gaze to the rolled-up newspaper and the way Brian had misspelled Olsen. I could grab a pen. Scribble it out and write it over. Let the Olsens know somebody noticed and somebody cared.

Or I could pretend I never saw it. I could let it slip by like the dozens of little mistakes that had earmarked this entire summer—not to mention the category-five catastrophes.

I tossed the mail onto the shelf with the other deliveries. "Screw it," I mumbled. Nothing was the same anymore. Why not embrace the fact?

Tommy's being gone was a clean slate, in a way. A fresh start. I knew all about fresh starts. A new foster home full of new possibilities and an uncomfortable room full of strangers and a bed I got to share with a girl who didn't like me. Also, she wasn't about to let me use her hair dryer or her brushes, and I didn't have my own, so my hair was always a disaster.

But I'd finally figured it out. Change—this thing I'd always hated and hoped to banish from my life—was the only thing I'd actually been able to count on. Broken dreams were my oldest friend. Darkness was the foundation to my entire existence.

I could trust these things. At least they were honest with me. At least I knew they would never abandon me.

And where did a dad fit into all this? Or a grandpa, for that matter?

Nowhere.

Nowhere at all.

I snapped a rubber band around another newspaper and didn't even check to see if Brian had spelled *Alsbach* right.

CHAPTER SEVEN
ANGELICA

———◈———

Head in her hand, elbow on a broad, round table, Angelica leaned over a newspaper, its spine protected by a wooden dowel. Light spilled across the yellowed page, pouring in from the picture windows that made up the southern wall of the Lake Geneva Public Library. The view of the lakefront was pristine, providing brief escapes when she thought her head and her heart could take no more. Shifting to rest her chin in her palm, she let her eyes rove for the hundredth time.

Down the shore to the left, a brick building with a pointed roof and stubby corner towers stood on the shore. A fleet of navy-and-white cruise boats sat at the piers below it, occasionally coming and going. She could hear their horns and whistles from anywhere downtown. Children played in the water at a little beach, their laughter drifting through the glass. The sound reminded her of her own boys back home, playing on much larger beaches, splashing through much larger waves, and she smiled. They were in good hands back home with her parents, but she missed them so much.

She'd been coming to the library every day for four days, hunting down articles from all the local and regional papers. Anything to do with the Markham Ring. Anything to do with the Geissler family of Chicago and Lake Geneva. Anything to do with Will. The articles all called him Fritz. But she had promised her hand and heart to Will Read, a man she was gradually accepting had never existed.

"Will" was from Grand Rapids, Michigan, or so he had told her. His father had been abusive and that was why Will had left for California, why he had never spoken of his past. Out of respect for this supposed pain, Angelica had rarely pushed him to talk about it, beyond the brief glimpses he offered, though reluctantly. And now she knew why.

They were all lies.

Fritz Geissler, on the other hand, had been born in Chicago in 1969. His parents owned real estate in the city and were considerably well-off. Well-off enough to own a mansion on the south shore of Geneva Lake. That's where Fritz had spent his summers as a child.

Angelica drank the information in like an alcoholic drank wine—knowing on some level that it was hurting her, but unable to stop. She would deal with the pain these articles provided by drinking in more of them. By crying alone in her hotel room at night. By staring at the ceiling, feeling hollowed out like a shell and asking a thousand more questions. Once she had drained the newspapers dry, and any other source she found, once she could soak in no more, perhaps her heart could finally heal.

Turning a page from 1986, she found a photo of Fritz. Thinking of him by his real name felt awkward, as if she were researching someone other than her husband. But it was easier that way. Fritz was the boy from Lake Geneva. Will was the man she had married. For now, the two weren't actually related.

In the photo, Fritz was seventeen years old, standing on a pier with two other boys, one of whom was holding a trophy. Behind them, a sailboat was tethered to the pier. The headline declared that they'd just taken first place in a regatta.

Angelica stroked the outline of the boy's face, fascinated by how similar he looked to her Will, by how much her older son Kaydon was destined to look like him in a few years. She studied the boat moored in the background. Fritz liked to sail? She and Will had lived so close to the ocean in Malibu. Why had they never bought a boat? Why had Will never felt drawn to the water, beyond taking his boys to swim on the weekends?

How could a man box up an entire past as if it had never existed? How could he not only lie to her, but also turn his back on everyone he had ever known—his friends, his family? How did a person do a thing like that? Why had he never told her *any* of this?

She studied the other two boys in the photograph. By now, she'd seen them so many times, she could recognize them by face: Jason Thomlin and Bobby Markham, her husband's childhood friends—and later, his companions in crime.

The articles covering the Markham Ring had dissected every aspect of their pasts. She now knew that these boys had grown up together. Gone to college together. Gotten jobs together at Bobby's father's bank. And together, they'd used what they knew of bank security to break into banks all over Chicago, Milwaukee, and Madison. The papers speculated they were responsible for the loss of millions of dollars. They also named Bobby the ringleader, thus the development of the name "Markham Ring," which was eventually applied after the ring was broken, right here in Lake Geneva. Their last job had been interrupted by the local police. There had been a shootout. Bobby had been killed. Jason and Fritz had fled.

That was the same summer that Will had moved to Los Angeles.

She couldn't begin to imagine how he had completely transformed his identity. How he had literally become another man.

Nor could she understand what would inspire Will—the Will she had known—to be involved in such a crazy thing. He and Bobby had both come from wealthy families while Jason was comfortably middle-class. All three boys were college-educated and had gotten good, lucrative jobs where they were promoted quickly. She knew little yet of Bobby and Jason and what may have motivated them. But Will?

She had shared a life with him. He was hard-working. He was kind. Above all, he was honest. To a fault. His most-valued ethic was to deal straight with every human being he met, whether a client, an employee, his sons, or his wife. He couldn't be five minutes late home from work without explaining to her the exact reason why. And she still remembered the soul-wrenching honesty with which he'd confessed about forgetting to take out the trash. She'd thought his nervous habit was habituated from fears of his father's abuse.

Now she wondered if Will was just overcompensating for the wreck of lies that trailed his wake. As if he feared that one day, Angelica would suddenly stop believing him.

Had their marriage in fact been that fragile? Had they always been a breath from failure? Had Will been the only one who'd even known it? Had he lived in fear of someday tipping his hand, giving up the game, and losing the picture-perfect life he'd gotten away with?

Tears welled in her eyes for the thousandth time since she'd gotten to Lake Geneva. She'd learned to keep a packet of tissues in her purse. But now she didn't care. She stretched her arms across the newspaper and flopped her head down. She let the tears run. Let them fall to the pages, where they would leave smeared ink and raised welts.

"Are you all right?"

The voice came in a whisper, appropriate for a library. She lifted her head and found an old man leaning over her, his sparse white hair combed over his scalp, one hand tucked into the pocket of a dusty-blue knitted cardigan. In his other hand, he held a heavy, hardback book. She glimpsed the title. *American Prometheus.* The cover showed the gaunt face of the man who had invented the atomic bomb.

She wiped the tears from her face. "Yes." She dug in her purse for the tissues, but before she could find them, the man handed her a crisp white handkerchief. The corner was embroidered in red thread with a coat of arms. Surprised by the offer, she took the handkerchief nonetheless and dabbed her eyes. "Thank you."

"Oh, don't mention it," the man said. "Is there anything I can do for you? Anything you need?"

She shook her head. "No, it's fine."

"You're new in town." He said it as an observation, not a question.

She furrowed her brow. "How do you know?" Who was this man? Was he stalking her? Fear rose in her throat. Why would someone want to stalk her?

"Oh, well—" He checked his watch. "It's late on a Saturday afternoon, and the tourists generally find more exciting distractions than the library and past editions of the *Lake Geneva Regional News.*" He motioned to the paper. "Did you just move here? Are you looking for work?"

"No." She folded the newspaper quickly and smoothed it down. She was beginning to wish he would go away. She didn't need friendly locals prying into her business—knowing who she was and why she was here.

But the man held up a hand to stay her. "I'm sorry. I really am being very clumsy. You see, I couldn't help but notice. You were looking at a photo of my son."

Angelica's ears perked. He... he knew one of the boys in the photo? Which one? Will? Adrenalin began to surge through her body. What was lies? What was truth? Could this be Will's father?

"Your son?" she asked, annoyance replaced with thrill and terror.

The man opened the page again and pointed to the young man in the middle, holding the sailing trophy. "That's him," he said. "Bobby. He was a very good sailor. All these boys were." He laughed. "Well, that's obvious. They won the regatta."

Not Will's father, but Bobby's. Angelica's heart pounded nonetheless, perhaps in relief. This was no time to finally meet her in-laws.

But it *was* the time to find answers, and Bobby's father might hold the ends of a thousand threads. This was the man who gave them all jobs at the First National Bank of Chicago. Until this moment, he had been a name in ink. Now here he was, living and breathing. She hadn't really had a mental image of what he should look like, but she had perhaps pictured someone with broad shoulders in a well-pressed suit, not a quiet old man in an oversized cardigan.

Her voice trembled as she asked, "Did you know the other boys, too?"

"Fritz and Jason?" The man looked through the window toward the lake and his eyes turned cloudy and distant, as if dwelling on long-ago memories. "They were like second sons to me. They practically grew up under my roof."

A lump rose in her throat, threatening to choke her. Tears watered her vision once again. Suddenly, the voices of the children on the beach became the long-ago voices of Bobby, Jason, and Fritz.

"Why?" the man asked. "Did you know them?"

She found herself nodding. "Fritz was my husband." Saying it with his real name felt strange. Like she was admitting to an affair.

But to her surprise, saying his name out loud—and tying herself to it—rolled a weight off her chest. No one in this town knew why she was here. She kept conversations short. Avoided eye contact. What would anyone think if the wife of one of their most infamous criminals showed up? Perhaps she shouldn't have told even Bobby's father.

But his face lit up. He dropped into the chair beside her, laying his book on the table, and took her hand in both of his. "My dear girl, I'm so delighted to meet you."

Angelica's uncertainty wavered into a smile. He welcomed her? Relief slowly trickled through her veins.

The old man's smile faded as he looked deeply into her eyes. "You never knew, did you? About... all this?" He waved his hand vaguely over the paper, the window, the lake, as if referring to a greater whole so vast, it defied brevity. "Lake Geneva. Your husband's life here. That's why you're here at the library, reading dusty old newspapers, isn't it?"

She nodded. Tears pricked her eyes. Embarrassed, she dipped her head and dried them with the handkerchief.

"Oh, my dear child." His crystal-blue eyes filled with sympathy.

His look, the tone of his voice—together they triggered that vulnerable place that continually threatened to erupt without warning. When she was cleaning the sheets and found a strand of Will's hair. When she was watching the sun set over the ocean, alone. When she was just trying to choose a bunch of tomatoes in the grocery store.

The newsprint in front of her blurred. Her throat constricted. Then the flood burst out, and she buried her sobs in the handkerchief.

The old man sat in silence, letting her cry. He didn't seem put off by her emotion. His quiet company was comforting, even. Her parents and her dear aunt and uncle, even her brothers and sisters and her cousins, would have been more boisterous, convinced the way to banish tears was to drown them in hugs and talk about what a bastard Will was and force quesadillas on her. But this man's wrinkled hand on hers was more than enough. She hadn't realized how badly she simply longed for a sympathetic face. Quiet company.

When she could breathe normally again, the old man spoke. "I can't begin to imagine what you've been through." He lifted his eyebrows and nodded. "You're very brave to come here and do this."

Angelica forced a smile and toyed with the edge of his handkerchief.

"I want you to know... Even after everything that happened, I never stopped thinking about Fritz and Jason. Wondering where they were. Hoping life was treating them kindly." He smiled at Angelica. "I see it did for Fritz."

She lowered her chin, offering a half-hearted grin in return for the compliment. Yes, perhaps life had treated Will kindly. But at her expense. Where she came from, *familia* was everything. You did not betray your family.

The man sat up abruptly. "Are you free tonight? I would be delighted if you joined me for dinner. You can ask me anything. I'm sure I knew Fritz as well as anyone around these parts. And I must admit, I'd be thrilled to get to know the woman he married."

She parted her lips, seeking an answer. Yes, she wanted this so much. But was she ready? If reading newspapers in the library had been like tippling drinks all day, going to dinner with Bobby's father would be like throwing back shots.

"We can go to Anthony's," he went on, then checked his watch. "The rush will have started, but they'll get me a table. They always do. The staff are superb. It'll all go on my tab, of course."

Angelica smiled, humored and enchanted by his eagerness. Would she be stupid to say no? What if she never saw this man again? The newspapers could only offer cold reality and harsh facts. Here was someone flesh-and-blood who had known her husband as a person.

She made up her mind. "Yes. Yes, I will have dinner with you. It would be my pleasure."

The man smiled. "Excellent." He offered his hand. "My name is Roland. Roland Markham."

She accepted the shake. "Angelica Read." She smiled. "I'm very glad to meet you."

CHAPTER EIGHT
ANGELICA

Angelica laughed over her Merlot. Their waiter had cleared the plates two hours ago and filled their third round of drinks, and Roland had not yet run out of tales with which to regale her. Bobby, Jason, and Fritz had been inseparable, sunup to sundown all summer long, and the return to school and the city at the end of the year was considered a great tragedy. Jason alone stayed at the lake, since his father worked for the cruise line, and the other boys counted him lucky.

Angelica set down her wine and leaned back in the luxurious, leather-trimmed captain's chair. She let her eyes rove over the paneled wood, the dim wall sconces, and time-darkened mirrors. Like Roland himself, Anthony's exuded the feeling of old money and the kind of grace, luxury, and etiquette one would have expected in the days of Audrey Hepburn and Cary Grant. What better place for time travel than a place like this, frozen in time?

Her eyes were finally out of tears—this time from laughing. She'd never thought she'd be able to laugh about her husband's past. But Roland had managed to keep the

41

evening light, every memory a treasure. His love for these boys and this lake was palpable. Overwhelming.

Bobby had been the gregarious one, often leading the children on their wildest of adventures. Jason had been a capable first mate and Fritz their loyal crew. She could see it so clearly now, how the quiet but loyal boy Fritz had later developed into the calm, considerate man Will.

But what had happened in between? How had the metamorphosis happened? All night, Roland had carefully avoided any mention of the ring. His son's death. The night Fritz and Jason had run away.

Angelica breathed deeply. She had come here for hard truths. She couldn't put them off forever. The time was now.

"Roland," she said, meeting his clear blue eyes, letting him know she was taking the conversation down a notch. She dipped her chin. "It was your pier, wasn't it?"

He stared at her, jaw loose, hands fidgeting with his wine glass, eyes darting away almost imperceptibly, as if seeking to avoid this part of the story. They had spoken all night of youth and vigor. Of course, he didn't want to speak of her husband's murder, just three weeks ago.

Angelica shook her head. "You don't need to deny it. I already saw it in the papers. Will's body was left at the end of your pier."

Roland released his breath and nodded. "Yes. That's true."

"Were you the one who found him?"

He shook his head. "No. It was one of the mail jumpers." He had already explained how Jason's father, Tommy Thomlin, drove the locally-famous Lake Geneva Mailboat. "She fell in, and..." He turned up his hands. "There he was."

Angelica didn't blink. Didn't waiver. There was time for tears, and there was time for truth. This was a time for truth. She forced her breath to remain steady. "Why? Why would he be left at your pier?"

Roland laid his linen napkin on the table and stroked the hem. "Until we know who killed him, I doubt we'll know why he was left where he was."

"Are there no theories? Do *you* have no theories?"

"Well, there *was* a theory, but it now has some rather obvious holes in it. And now there's a new one." Roland grinned, acknowledging the amorphous nature of the case.

"What was the first theory?" She didn't care if it had been disproved. She needed to know everything. She didn't just need to know who her husband was and how he could have betrayed her. She needed to know who had killed him and why. Who had shattered the bubble of her perfect life. Who had slapped her awake and plunged her into cold water.

"The first theory is that Fritz was killed by my neighbor, Charles Hart."

Angelica frowned, searching her memory. "I've read his name. Where do I know his name?"

"He murdered Jason Thomlin, days after your husband was killed. Charles kidnapped Jason and then shot him. But Jason fought back. Charles died that night, as well."

Angelica nodded, the facts resurfacing from the many articles she had digested over the past four days. She had placed more emphasis on learning anything related to her husband and hadn't yet addressed the murder of his accomplice Jason. "And why would your neighbor want Jason and Will dead?"

Perhaps her eyes were tricked by the dim lighting, but she thought Roland blushed. "Well... Charles and I... We knew each other for years. Decades. He, ah..." Roland hesitated. "Well, he was married, but they were never precisely..."

Angelica narrowed her eyes. "You had an affair with his wife?" She didn't mean to be unfeeling. She just wanted the truth.

Roland blinked, genuinely surprised. "Wh—? No."

"He had an affair with yours?"

Roland stirred in his seat, frowning. "No, no, not at all."

Angelica mentally flipped through the remaining possibilities. Landing on one, she smiled knowingly. "He was gay."

Roland slouched and looked down, curling up inside himself. "Yes." He drummed his thumbs on the base of his wine glass.

Angelica raised an eyebrow and grinned. "He liked you?"

"Yes."

"But you didn't like him?"

He sat up a little straighter, a flustered bird ruffling its feathers. "Well, no."

Angelica thought she believed him. His neighbor's sexual orientation genuinely seemed to trouble him. She shook her head. Roland was from such another era. "So, why would he kill Jason and Will?"

Roland shifted in his seat, continuing to appear uncomfortable. "Perhaps I railed against Jason and Fritz one too many times..."

She frowned. "What do you mean?" Despite what they had done, Roland claimed to be full of nothing but love toward the boys. After listening to dozens of his tales, she truly believed it.

He couldn't seem to meet her eyes. "At one time, I may have felt that they... er... had some hand in turning Bobby astray."

Her frown only deepened. "You said Bobby led the shenanigans."

"Burgling banks isn't exactly shenanigans."

"They named the ring after *him*. The Markham Ring." She wasn't sure why she was defending her husband. The man had lied to her. Maybe she was only clinging tenaciously to truth. There was no way, knowing what she knew, that Jason and Will had been the ring leaders.

Roland leaned back, raising his palms. "I only mean to say..." He drew in his breath and clenched his hands helplessly, then tilted his head and tried again. "You have children, Angelica."

She pictured her boys, Kaydon and Mason. If anyone accused them of a crime, wouldn't she defend them to her last breath? Hadn't she defended Will, until it was obvious she couldn't?

"I lost Bobby seventeen years ago and was as blindsided by the truth as you. I had dinner with them the night before they tried to rob the Grand Bank of Geneva. The next morning, the police told me they had shot him." He shrugged. "Anger needs an out, and Jason and Fritz had made themselves convenient scapegoats. They had fled. They would never even know how much blame I laid at their feet."

Angelica nodded. Perhaps she could understand. "And what do you believe now?"

He sighed and collapsed his hands on the table in front of him. "I believe it becomes harder to fight the truth. Which means I'm not sure how I..." He lifted his eyes to stare across the room, and to Angelica's surprise, they glistened. "I *thought* I raised him well." The hopelessness hung in every word.

She let it soak in and again thought of her boys. How would she feel if, after the countless hours of love and devotion she'd poured into them, they turned their backs on everything she had taught them? Would it be easier to blame someone else than to face the fear that you had failed your own child?

She didn't want Roland to spin off into despair. Questions like these—did they ever have answers? "Charles clearly believed Fritz and Jason were more culpable than Bobby."

Roland laughed softly and stared at his hands. "Yes, I suppose he must have."

45

"And that's why he avenged your son's death?"

Roland shrugged. "So the theory goes. Now that he's gone, we can never really know. But why else would he have killed Jason?" He lifted a finger. "Keep in mind—while he has been officially accused of Jason's murder, he's not been accused of Fritz's." He shrugged. "Granted, I'm sure the police have more information than gets into the press, but if he were guilty, wouldn't they have said? Rather, by all accounts, they appear to still be looking."

Angelica nodded. It seemed cosmically unfair that Jason's murder should be solved while her husband's was left a blank page. Was anyone even investigating? It had been so long since she'd heard anything from the police...

She pushed on. "You said this theory has holes in it. That there's a second theory. What is it?"

"That there was a fourth member of the Markham Ring."

Angelica frowned. "A fourth member?"

Roland nodded. "Charles wasn't alone the night he murdered Jason. There was a witness to the crime, and according to her, there was an accomplice. A man who took part in Jason's murder. A man who got away."

"They haven't caught him yet?"

"No. I'm not sure they so much as have a clue as to his identity."

"But he was working with Charles."

"Clearly."

"Then there were five members. Charles was in on it."

"At the very least, Charles had to have been aware of what he was doing and who he was dealing with."

"Why do they believe there were more members of the ring? Why didn't Charles maybe have a friend helping him with his revenge pact? A hired gun, even?"

"Because the violence didn't end with Charles' death. A week later, Jason's father was shot."

Angelica sat up straighter. "Tommy Thomlin, the boat captain?"

"He survived," Roland assured her. "But I haven't heard he was able to identify the villain."

Angelica shook her head. "But why go after Jason's father?"

Roland shrugged. "Because he thought Tommy knew something? You must admit, it's the best theory available so far."

Angelica narrowed her eyes. "And why would this fourth member leave my husband's body at the end of your pier?" A thought clicked into place and her eyes widened. "As a warning? Roland, you aren't in danger, are you?"

Roland looked away, rolling his head as if annoyed. "Oh, the police insist I am."

"And?"

"And it's been three weeks. Yet here I am."

It was a fair point. Still, Angelica wasn't sure if Roland was being brazen or just naive. After all, Tommy Thomlin had been shot.

Roland lifted his glass. "Angelica, this conversation has grown too morbid. You'll never be able to sleep tonight. Let's change the subject. Come, now. What else do you want to know about Lake Geneva?"

Reluctantly, Angelica picked up her glass and sipped her wine. She'd let Roland ramble about days gone by. She would smile. She would laugh. She would treasure every memory. But in the back of her mind, she would turn over everything Roland had told her about her husband's death. She couldn't tolerate the vacuum of answers. She wouldn't let Will's murder go unsolved.

CHAPTER NINE
SKULL

———————⚓———————

In a corner booth, a man dined alone. He'd combed the usual care-free spikes out of his hair, styling it into something more suave and sophisticated. The full tattoo sleeves down his arms were concealed by the white button-down shirt. Some jobs required him to put his ink under wraps. Images such as the cracked skull with the rose adorning its forehead didn't exactly fit in at Anthony's.

He was known for that tattoo. His buddies called him Skull.

The Man paid good money for him to blend in—and good enough money for Skull to order a forty-dollar steak. The job was beyond easy—for now. All he was supposed to do was sit and watch for a woman named Angelica Read. He would recognize her as a petite Hispanic woman with long black hair, fashionable style sense, and a light Mexican accent.

And just like The Man had said, there she was, sitting with none other than Roland Markham, wining and dining the night away. The bug he had dropped in her purse in passing fed every word of their conversation into an invisible piece in his left ear. When she left, it would track her location.

Regardless, he was to never let her out of his sight.

It was worth getting in a good meal now. Running surveillance without backup was a demanding job. But Skull was used to it. Discreet information was his business. And the only other person in on the contract, Bud Weber, was both an idiot and out of The Man's graces. That's what you got for insubordination. In a game like this, you didn't run around following personal vendettas, shooting targets that weren't included in The Plan. Bud had taken offense to Jason's father, Tommy Thomlin, for being a decent human being. The boat captain had reported that Weber beat his foster child, and that raised Weber's ire. Well, Bud shouldn't have touched the girl in the first place. Getting arrested on an unrelated charge could ruin everything. And The Man would be none too pleased.

At one time, Skull wondered why The Man kept Weber around at all, but eventually the answers came clear. Bud was a good gun. He could keep a crime scene pristine. He had a sixth sense that kept him both alive and beyond the reach of the law. Once you understood how many murders Bud had committed—and gotten away with—you understood why he had been on the contract.

But most importantly, The Man thrived on people he could manipulate. And Bud was nothing if not manipulable, just as Charles Hart had been. When working with The Man, you couldn't show emotion. Not without exposing yourself to him. He would use you every bit as much as he did his victims. The Man always got what he wanted.

There was only one other person on the team, a brilliant teenage boy named Baron Hackett. He was currently serving time, however—a move that had been carefully planned and executed. The boy would be out soon; his impeccable behavior behind bars was also carefully planned. There was an accomplice Skull would have trusted. But that didn't help Skull tonight. He'd have to do everything solo. So long as Angelica didn't become suspicious of him, it shouldn't be a problem.

And the subjects of his inquiries never became suspicious.

Roland Markham and Angelica Read finally rose from their table. Skull gave them a few minutes, then casually followed. He stopped outside the door to light a cigarette, noting that Roland and Angelica were still talking next to their cars. Their conversation buzzed in his ear, but it was meaningless. He would smoke and enjoy the evening, and if they talked long, he would pull out his phone and pretend to make a call.

But the two hugged goodnight and got into their own vehicles.

Skull dropped his cigarette and ground it under his toe. He made his way casually to his car. It was late, and in all likelihood, Angelica would go straight to her hotel. If she did, he'd learn what room she was in, then try to get one nearby. In the morning, he would be up early, ready to follow her wherever she went.

The Man couldn't manipulate his victims without knowing every last detail about them. Luckily, being nosy was Skull's specialty.

MONDAY
JULY 14, 2014

CHAPTER TEN
MONICA

My pen flew across my legal pad, disjointed thoughts racing out of my mind. I wrote names. I wrote dates. I wrote theoretic connections between people. I asked questions. I suggested leads to follow up on. I ground my forehead into the hand supporting it, wracking my brain for answers.

Who was The Man Upstairs?

The second-floor meeting room at the LGPD buzzed with half-sleepy, nine-in-the-morning conversation. The air smelled of fresh-brewed coffee, donuts, various brands of shampoo and aftershave, paper and ink, and the electricity from the projector. People were dressed in suits and ties, or in slacks and polo shirts like me. They all carried a service weapon on their hip. I could identify the badges of half a dozen departments—Walworth County Sheriff's Office, as a matter of course; a humbling array of nearby city and county principalities which had volunteered their personnel and resources; and one agent each from the Wisconsin Department of Criminal Investigations, the FBI, and the ATF.

After three homicides, a shooting, and a bombing—all in the course of two weeks—the workload was simply more than Lehman, Neumiller, and I could handle on our own. So we'd formed an investigative task force and invited the entire cavalry. For the most part, we weren't even sure yet what we were investigating. Why had the surviving members of the Markham Ring been murdered? Why were near family apparently being targeted, as well? Jason's father, Tommy Thomlin, had been shot, while Bobby's father, Roland Markham had been warned.

And then a boy named Jimmy Beacon had detonated a bomb in the middle of downtown on the Fourth of July. The incident wouldn't have been related at all, except for that anonymous phone call I'd gotten afterwards. Someone calling himself The Man Upstairs. Someone claiming to be behind it all, the bombing included. Someone saying he knew the town's deepest secrets.

Including mine.

I frowned at my tangled swamp of notes. Finding The Man himself wasn't *supposed* to be my part of the investigation. I was assigned to follow up on Fritz Geissler, the first murder victim.

I snorted. Like hell I was going to leave it alone. I wasn't going to let someone get under my skin like that.

My partner, Stan Lehman, stepped behind the desk at the front of the room. "Good morning, good morning," he said, tapping a stack of papers together loudly.

Members of the task force grabbed last-minute muffins and cups of coffee, then migrated toward their seats. Metal chair legs clanged against tables. People flowed around me like a herd of cows, while I was a rock in the middle, already at my desk. I frowned down at my black leather portfolio and the yellow legal pad inside. The page looked like the ravings of a madwoman. Maybe they were.

Mark Neumiller, my other partner in the LGPD Detective Bureau, pulled up a chair beside me and set down a notebook and a paper cup full of water from the cooler. I flipped the cover of my portfolio to conceal what I'd been working on and turned my attention to the front of the room.

Leadership of the task force had fallen to Lehman, as Detective Sergeant of the department where the case had originated. To colleagues who only knew us marginally, it had apparently come as a surprise that Lehman held rank over me. Based on their expressions, it was even more stunning that I could sit amongst the rank and file and take orders from someone else. Even in passing, I tended to form a reputation as a strong woman. (Read that "bitch.") But I didn't like people well enough to lead them. Lehman could have that job. Besides, in our bureau, we knew who really wore the pants.

Lehman picked up a marker from the whiteboard tray and glanced over his notes, scrawled in a first-grader's handwriting. While we all had access to a database containing every detail of the case, Lehman still insisted on his color-coded note system. No one else bothered to reference it, especially as new notes in unestablished colors were squeezed in at odd angles. So far as I could tell, Lehman just wanted to play with markers while looking important.

"Okay," he said, popping the marker cap on and off. "Neumiller, Thompson, how are we doing on Amelia Beacon's case?"

Mark Neumiller had partnered up with Detective Al Thompson from Racine PD to investigate that angle. Before detonating his bomb, Jimmy Beacon had accused his boss, Bud Weber, of murdering his little sister years ago when his family lived in Racine. Weber had been interrogated twenty ways to Sunday that night. He'd admitted to living in the same city at that time, but maintained his innocence, even refusing a lawyer. But it didn't help his case that he'd been recently under investigation for allegedly abusing his foster child, Bailey Johnson. We were merely looking for the chink in the story that would blow it all apart.

Neumiller sipped his water and glanced over his notes. "We've been to the apartment complex where Weber lived. It's literally ten minutes from the playground where Amelia was kidnapped."

"Weber declined a voluntary DNA swab?"

"That's right."

"Can we court order him yet?"

Neumiller shook his head. "I've hashed that over with the DA. He doesn't think the judge will go for it without more evidence."

I tapped my foot impatiently. Suspicions and proof were two different things, and the gray zone in between was where scum like Bud Weber thrived and did their dirty work.

"We're talking to the landlord and the neighbors," Neumiller went on, "trying to dig up Bud's friends and figure out if we can confirm a location for Weber that day. His reference swore Bud was at work. Bud's employer said he might be able to produce records of who was on shift that day and when. He's just got some digging to do."

"That's a good lead. Do we know where Jimmy got the pink bow?"

Witnesses on the day of the bombing claimed Jimmy had confronted Bud with a pink bow, which he claimed his sister had been wearing the day she disappeared. Later, we found remnants of pink polyester satin in the blast zone.

Neumiller shook his head again. "No one ever saw him with it until he displayed it to Weber."

"Who, of course, never saw it in his life..." Lehman's sarcastic comment trailed off as he added new notes to his marker board. "Anything else?"

"Nope. We'll keep you posted."

Footwork. Rock-turning. Haystack-poking. Paper pushing. Those words described the nature of the entire investigation. It wasn't that we had a lack of leads; it was that we had too many, and yet not enough. Every tiny fact could prove pointless, or it could be the clue we so desperately needed to unravel the entire case.

There was a subdued vibration in the air that was palpable. Our focus was controlled, intense. I'd once seen a bloodhound track a scent for thirty miles on winding county highways, never giving up, never forgetting what he was after, never being distracted by irrelevant scents. That was us. At the end of the trail, there *would* be arrests, at least two of them—Bud Weber and The Man Upstairs.

Lehman twiddled his marker. "All right. Let's talk about God. I mean, The Man Upstairs."

People snickered. But I leaned on my hand to shield my face from the room. I didn't need my cheeks to flush. Every time The Man came up in discussion, I felt exposed. Vulnerable. Afraid of what my unknown nemesis knew. Equally afraid of what my colleagues might find out. The men and women of the Lake Geneva Police were something like family to me. But to this day, not one of them knew about my baby or my abortion. It was a side of me I'd never shown. A side I was still hopeful never to reveal. No one belonged in that sanctuary of pain and confusion but me.

So how had The Man Upstairs gotten in? I had questions. And I had ideas on how to find the answer.

Lehman was still talking. "Hayworth, you were cleaning up that audio file. Did you get anything?"

Detective Adam Hayworth from Walworth County tapped the touchpad on his laptop. "I don't know what he did to conceal his voice. I haven't been able to strip it out yet." He frowned at his screen. "But I managed to pick out some noises in the background. Listen to this."

He clicked his mouse again. Sound came from a USB speaker plugged into his laptop.

"I even know how to exploit your children," the rasping voice said—the one I couldn't get out of my dreams at night. *"Yes, Monica. YOUR children."*

Hayworth had clearly rebalanced the sound to emphasize the background. But all I heard was the voice. Taunting me. Challenging me. Whispering to me. *I know you were going to have a child. And I know you ended the pregnancy without even telling your husband. And I know how badly you want to protect that information...*

The first time Lehman had played the recording for the task force, half the room had turned to look at me. They knew I didn't have kids.

"There's, ah... There's nothing personal to that, right?" Lehman had asked uncomfortably.

"No," I snapped back. And since that was my usual tone of voice, no one had questioned me further.

Maybe even *I* was paranoid. Children? There had only been one pregnancy, one fetus. Had The Man really been suggesting he had information on me personally? If so, it was bad information.

Or had he used the plural on purpose? To keep me guessing? Doubting? Underestimating my opponent? Was he inviting me to assume he was stupid? He claimed to know the deepest secrets of the entire town. Did he *want* me to think he didn't?

I shot breath through my nose. This was why I couldn't sleep at night. Why the bullet journal in my ledger was more like the chalk on the walls drawn by an inmate at an asylum for the insane.

As Hayworth played the audio again now, I bit my lip and forced myself to concentrate. I had to catch this guy. I had to catch him...

A rhythmic ticking sounded quietly in the background noises that Hayworth had isolated.

"That's a clock," Lehman observed.

"So he made the call indoors in a room with a clock," Neumiller concluded. Pens scribbled around the room and keyboards clicked.

"An old clock," Hayworth added. "I haven't fully isolated this sound yet, but you can just hear the gears turning, and then—there. That was the clock striking the quarter hour."

"The Man Upstairs hangs out with Father Time," quipped a young detective from Janesville. The room laughed.

"So, is this a grandfather clock? A wall clock? A mantle clock?" asked Lehman.

Hayworth shook his head. "Sounds old. Mechanical, obviously. I have an appointment with a clockmaker this afternoon. I'll run it past him and see what he knows."

It would have been far more helpful to pick out a Harley Davidson idling in the driveway, or better yet, a recorded voice for the blind saying that it was safe to cross name-of-street now. Something that could help us identify the location from *outside.* With the audio of the clock, all we could do was verify we had the right place *after* we'd found it and physically been *inside.* Good stuff if this all came to trial—but the slow boat to China while we were still trying to find the place.

But if the clockmaker was good—and if clocks could, in fact, be identified merely by their sound—we could turn more stones. If it was a rare antique, we could possibly create a list of those clocks still in existence. From there, it would be a matter of tracking down every single one until we found an owner and a location that might fit the case.

This was the nature of the evidence we had to work with. It was going to be a long, long road. Normally, this was the kind of tedious, OCD work I thrived on.

But it was hard to focus on the details when I heard The Man's voice screaming in the back of my head day and night. I wanted him behind bars *now.*

Lehman's marker squeaked across the board, leaving a trail of orange. "Were you able to pick out anything else? Traffic? Other voices?"

Hayworth shook his head. "Just the clock."

Lehman nodded. "All right. Well. Let us know if you make any more progress on the disguised voice."

"Will do."

Lehman capped his orange marker. "Okay. What else? Oh, right. Brandt. You turned up something on the abuse case. Bailey Johnson. Why don't you fill us in?"

People shifted in their seats to face Ryan. He sat near the door, dressed in a patrolman's uniform—navy blue, almost dark enough to be black. The lack of reflective striping, royal blue yoke, and cargo shorts meant he wasn't on bike patrol today. Still, this was the first I'd ever heard of a seasonal bike patrol officer getting a seat in an investigative task force. But in the earliest days of the case, Lehman, Neumiller, and I had been strapped with the murder investigations. So Ryan had ended up spearheading the investigation into Bud Weber, Jimmy's boss and Bailey's foster dad. Ryan had a rapport with Bailey, plus plenty of past experience as a detective, and that had landed him the project. Even after the case had grown, the task force had seen no reason not to let him continue his investigation on Weber. The chief had promised to allow for room in his schedule.

Before Ryan could speak, Lehman added, "Oh, and congrats on the promotion."

Neumiller leaned back in his chair to address the room. "He's permanent now," he announced.

The room applauded politely and a few hands thumped Ryan on the back. He grinned appreciatively.

So it had happened, then. Ryan was year-round. Dammit. I gripped my pen so tightly, I felt plastic crackle. I'd sworn I'd leave if he stayed. Would I? With a case like this on my hands? With a madman toying with the intimate details of my life?

Ryan stood, staring at a printout in his hand. "Okay. I don't have a lot. I mean—" he lifted the paper. "I found this half an hour before the meeting started."

Maybe Wade "making room" in Ryan's schedule was a little too generous an expression.

Ryan scratched his head, scanning the writing. "Anyway, Bud Weber is listed as a witness in regard to a murder that took place in downtown Chicago on October 29, 1994."

"Who was the victim?" asked Lehman.

"Zayne Mars," Ryan read. "Male, twenty-one years of age. He was Bud's roommate."

Lehman paused, purple marker hovering. "And you say Bud was a witness? Not a suspect?"

Ryan scanned the report again. "Yeah." He shrugged. "Go figure."

A few detectives smothered laughter. There was no love lost around here on Bud Weber.

"Anything else?" Lehman asked.

"No, just that." Ryan shrugged as he sat down. "I'm heading to his bar after the meeting to see what I can learn."

"Okay. Interesting lead. Keep us posted." Lehman twiddled the marker. "Who's next? Tolsky, you were piecing together a timeline for Jason Thomlin. What've you got?"

I sat through another hour of reports, jotting the occasional note, bouncing my foot, itching to get out of this meeting room and back on the street. Lehman and I planned to speak with the staff at the Abbey Resort in Fontana. We now had all of Fritz Geissler's phone and Internet data as well as his bank records. With that, we'd pieced together a timeline of exactly where he'd been and when, from the day he flew out of Los Angeles to the day he was murdered in Lake Geneva. He'd spent his last night on earth at the Abbey Resort. We wanted to talk with the staff to see what they knew and if he met anyone while he was there.

Anyone like The Man Upstairs.

The sooner we caught the bastard behind all this, the sooner I could sit him in a chair and demand an answer out of him.

How did you know?

"All right," Lehman said. "Good work, everybody. You all have your assignments. We meet again tomorrow, same time, same place. Good luck."

Chairs bumped over carpeted floor. Conversations resumed. Notes were compared in more detail. Empty coffee cups were thrown into the trash can by the door, Styrofoam gliding down the filmy trash can liner.

I closed my portfolio and made for the escape, avoiding eye contact with anyone in the room. I didn't need questions. I'd recorded my conversation with The Man Upstairs and I'd shared it with the task force. I'd been a very good girl, sharing it at all. I didn't need to be taken off the case because I was suddenly too close to it. Worse, I didn't need prying eyes and ears inside my personal business. I didn't need a whole crowd inside my confused and ravished heart. It had already been invaded. It had already been ransacked. I didn't...

I bit my lips so I wouldn't cry and sucked in air through my nose. I didn't need to fall apart in front of all my colleagues. Because fall apart was all I knew how to do when it came to the questions that clandestinely defined my life—the questions of what exactly I'd done ten years ago and why and if I should have waited until I was less furious with Ryan and if I should have told him.

Ryan. Against my bidding, my eyes flickered to him as I passed. He was looking at me, too. Of course he would be. I moved faster so he couldn't stop me. No, I didn't want to go out for drinks. No, I didn't want to talk about the case or his promotion or anything else on the face of the earth.

I just wanted to disappear. I wanted to feel safe again, all my secrets hidden where only I could find them, hold them, comfort them.

No one was supposed to be allowed in there.

CHAPTER ELEVEN
RYAN

———————————✦———————————

Pretending I was still invested in my conversation with Al Thompson from Racine, I watched out of the corner of my eye as Monica bolted from the room. She was avoiding me—nothing strange. But I wanted to know how she felt about me staying on. Was she upset? Was she going to resign? Unfortunately, I couldn't interpret her current level of snark any different from the usual.

I wished Lehman hadn't said anything. I'd wanted to tell her myself. Not necessarily to get her response; just to show her I was being up-front. Now I'd lost that chance. And with her bolting through the door, I'd lost the chance to apologize afterwards.

Regardless of her reaction, I was worried about her. I'd been watching her over the past week of these task force meetings, and I was beginning to see a pattern. Every time we got around to The Man Upstairs, she looked down. Got very busy with her notes. Looked uncomfortable. Why?

Granted, I'd be pretty pissed, too, if the unknown mastermind behind a string of murders had my cell number. I wanted to ask her if she'd changed it but didn't know how to do that without coming off creepy—you know, her ex making sure he was up-to-date on her phone number.

But knowing her, she wouldn't change it. She would tempt The Man Upstairs to bite again. She wanted to hear from him. She wanted to catch him. There was no criminal she feared to face.

But was she taking other precautions? Was her home secured? Did she park in well-lit areas? Did she keep her gun within reach at all times?

I could keep myself from following her around the room like a love-sick puppy. But keeping myself from worrying about her was a lost cause.

CHAPTER TWELVE
MONICA

From the meeting room, I breezed toward the stairwell, portfolio pressed to my chest, and unlocked the door with the key card in my hip pocket.

Lehman dashed out of the meeting room on my heels, fumbling a folder, his phone, and a set of car keys. He caught the door just before I let it swing shut on him. "Hey, all good?"

"Yeah, fine," I lied. "Ready for The Abbey?" I headed down the stairs, my shoes pounding every step as if to punish them.

"Yes, ma'am." I heard his fingers paging through the folder and pictured the sheets and colored sticky notes protruding in every direction. "Knowing how you're allergic to moss on your rear, I thought to grab everything I needed ahead of the meeting."

"Finally, some efficiency around here!" I spat back. The vitriol, of course, was not intended for him. But he was a convenient target.

I threw myself against the door at the bottom of the stairs and spilled out into the light of the July day.

Two men and one woman dressed in business casual were waiting, one with a TV camera on his shoulder, the others with digital cameras around their necks and notepads in their hands. Their swag was from three different media outlets. "Detective, a word!" They crowded toward me, starved dogs to an already-picked carcass.

"Jesus Christ," I muttered.

I felt Lehman behind me and heard him whisper in my ear. "Meet you at the car."

I took his offer of escape and pushed through the reporters, stiffening my back to warn them against messing with me.

"I'll take your questions," Lehman said, drawing their attention. Communicating with the media was his job anyway. But still, I owed him a solid for getting them off my back. While the media storm had died down in the week since the bombing, some hangers-on stuck like leeches, positive we were concealing information the public desperately needed to know. Turns out, setting off a bomb in a popular tourist town is a juicy story.

Over my shoulder, I heard them launch questions in rapid fire.

"Is there any connection between the bombing and the recent spate of murders?"

"What's the condition of the five individuals injured during the explosion?"

"Is there any evidence yet that Bud Weber murdered the bomber's sister?"

I huffed a sigh—then nearly walked head-first into a large woman stepping out from a park bench under a tree.

"Detective Steele," she cried in a ragged voice tarred by cigarettes, "I've been calling you all week."

I know, I almost replied, but bit my tongue.

Delilah Beacon's greasy hair hung in gray tatters around the shoulders of her drooping tee shirt. Her eyes were red with tears, and she reached for me with a crumpled tissue in her palm.

"Detective Steele, I buried my son yesterday," she went on. "I buried my Jimmy. I couldn't even have an open casket. They wouldn't even let me see my baby."

She wouldn't have deserved one anyway. When we asked her who her son spent time with, hoping to find a connection to The Man Upstairs, she couldn't give us a single name. She literally didn't know who her son's friends were. Turned out, he barely had friends at all. And she hadn't known that, either.

"Please, detective, why didn't you stop him? He was a good boy, really." Even as she spoke, her eyes flickered to the media and their cameras, a hungry look in her expression.

I bit back my rage. *You never cared a wit about your son, you attention whore.* Her son had been a child genius—isolated by his brilliance. But Delilah Beacon was incapable of being a mother long enough to notice. When we'd come to search her house, she'd told us we were welcome to take him. She couldn't wait for him to be off her hands. How did such a woman deserve the name of mother?

The familiar pain stabbed through my belly again. The long years of waiting. Of wanting. The soul-sucking thief—infertility. The child that was finally, beautifully mine, but whom I turned against on the same day I learned of her, for the sole sin of being her father's daughter.

I never would have hesitated to support another woman pursuing an abortion after her husband cheated on her. But never in a million years had I seen *me* making that choice. It was for other women with other problems. Not me. My marriage was beautiful. My life was promising. My family was finally going to be complete... And then I was slapped in the face with reality. Suddenly, I *was* "other women."

67

A woman who was hurt in the deepest way possible by the love of her life.

A woman who grabbed her choice feverishly and wielded it like a club.

But I was the one who took the blows.

Self-loathing pointed a gnarled finger in my face. *You're no better than Delilah Beacon.* The pain shot up my core into my face, twisting my mouth and brow.

One of the reporters glanced our way. Delilah didn't miss it. She grabbed my shirt and fell to her knees, like a saint from a Renaissance painting. Like she had a halo over her head and rivers of light pouring around her.

The feel of her body glued to mine shot terror up my back. What was wrong with me? How had I allowed her into my personal space? Every training video I'd ever watched of cops being grappled and killed flashed through my mind. I put one hand to my gun to head off the chance of her disarming me and tried to break away.

She wouldn't let go. My shirt tugged on my shoulders. "He didn't mean to," she wailed. "He was my son." I could almost feel her throwing an inviting wink to the reporters.

"Back off!" I said in a commanding tone, still trying to step away. I didn't dare touch her. The last thing I needed was a picture of me in the papers attacking the bomber's mother.

A manila envelope appeared out of nowhere, bristling with a rainbow of sticky notes. It slipped between me and Delilah Beacon.

"Hey, hey, hey," said Lehman. He firmly removed her hands from my shirt. "This is called assaulting an officer of the law. You can't do that."

Mrs. Beacon looked up at him with tearful eyes, hands clasped in prayerful innocence. "Are you going to arrest me, officer?"

Why did I think she would be delighted? Lehman clearly saw it, too, and wasn't about to give her the satisfaction.

"You harass Detective Steele one more time, and you will give me no other option. Now go about your business." He put a hand on my back and steered me toward the car. "Let's go."

I didn't waste time arguing. But I couldn't help looking over my shoulder. Mrs. Beacon was making a show of struggling weakly to her feet, wiping tears from her eyes. Meanwhile, the reporters were closing in on her, slow but eager, no one wishing to break propriety, no one wanting to be the last to a juicy source. In the end, they all arrived at the same time.

"Are you James Beacon's mother?" one of them asked.

She blinked tearfully, looking them up and down as if she hadn't noticed them until now. "I am," she said, twisting her tissue in her fingers.

"May we ask you some questions?"

"You have to understand, I'm still grieving." She dabbed her eyes.

The man with the video camera pushed to the front. "My channel will pay for an exclusive interview."

The other man shot him a dirty look. The woman reporter simply dug in her pocket. "My paper will pay, too! We'll give you a thousand dollars!"

And with that, the bidding war began. Delilah Beacon smiled. I knew in my gut she would take the highest bidder—then call the others later, claiming the deal had fallen through. She would collect her fee from them all and make bank off her son's story. And behind the reporters' backs, she would boast that Jimmy's death was the best thing that had ever happened to her.

"My God," I swore.

Lehman took my arm and forced my attention forward. "Just walk away," he said. "There's nothing you can do."

I clenched my fists and pushed a guttural scream through my teeth. Lehman was right, but that wasn't going to stop me from venting. Women like her didn't deserve to be mothers.

But neither did I. Given a second chance at motherhood? I would walk away. I had proved I wasn't deserving. Children didn't exist to be used by adults.

Lehman moved to the driver's side of our SUV, pulling keys out of his pocket. I crossed to the passenger side, scanning my surroundings as I reached for the door handle. I'd let my guard down, allowing myself to be surprised twice in a row, first by the press, then by Mrs. Beacon. I wasn't going to give Lehman the opportunity to rub my nose in that fact. Neither was I going to let it happen again.

That's when my gaze landed on a woman standing on the sidewalk across the street. Her eyes were hidden behind large sunglasses, but her whole face was centered on mine. Her skin was brown, her hair long and black. She wore a breezy white top and pale pink shorts. Her wide straw hat matched her straw handbag, which matched her beaded sandals.

I know you, my brain said. I squinted. *Where do I know you?* I met hundreds of people in my line of business, and it was vital I remember them all. Any one of them could prove an ally or an enemy at the drop of a pin. It disturbed me when I couldn't remember if I'd returned a person's stolen purse or called them because their kid was purse-snatching.

Moments passed, and she didn't look away. Her mouth remained a concrete line. Definitely an enemy, then. That made it all the more imperative I remember her name. And soon.

The engine turned. Lehman rolled down the window beside me. "Monica? You coming?"

70

I glanced at him. Hot air rolled through the window, hurried along by the AC Lehman had cranked up. "Yeah, coming."

I looked again, but the woman was walking down the street as if nothing had happened. I climbed into the passenger seat. I had the drive between here and The Abbey to try to remember who she was.

CHAPTER THIRTEEN
ANGELICA

———— ⚓ ————

Angelica Read clutched the strap of her straw handbag and pounded down the sidewalk. That woman... So much for avoiding Monica Steele. At least she didn't seem to recognize her. Angelica would never forget her.

Only three weeks ago, Detective Steele had shown up in Malibu, on her doorstep, and sat in her living room. In one breath, she'd offered her condolences for Will's passing. In the next, she'd demanded information on his criminal past—a past Angelica knew nothing about. Detective Steele had ripped off the blindfold and the Band-Aid, both at once, leaving Angelica reeling. Who did a thing like that? Angelica had just lost her husband. Her sons had lost their father. The woman was cold. Heartless.

Angelica bit her lip and fought back angry tears. No, she would not let this ruin her day. She would go on. She would keep searching for truth.

But if there was anyone she wished to avoid in this town, it was Monica Steele.

CHAPTER FOURTEEN
SKULL

———— ✪ ————

Leaning against a tree across the street from the police station, Skull dragged on his cigarette and exhaled a cloud of smoke. Today, he was dressed as a tourist. Tee shirt. Shorts. Baseball hat. Sunglasses. The rose skull could get some daylight this time. He'd sun-screened carefully to save the ink.

The vignette across the street was very interesting. Monica Steele and Angelica Read had crossed paths—and the tension was so thick, he could have sketched an idea for a new tattoo on it.

The Man would want to hear about this.

Of course, there was no love lost between Steele and Jimmy Beacon's mother, either. Skull would include that in the report, as well. Maybe The Man would bite; maybe he'd let that bait go without so much as a nibble. He was a wise old trout, hard to predict. Maybe he was tired of the Beacon family. Maybe he felt he'd already wrung every last drop of blood he could from them.

But Angelica Read? She was new. She was exciting. Or perhaps, despite appearances, the smooth socialite

Angelica was the woman more capable of destruction. After all, what The Man wanted was blood, plain and simple.

The Beacon woman was a glass of nitroglycerin, ready to explode at the trembling of a hand. So what was Read? Maybe a slow, steady boil. Maybe a jet of steam The Man could concentrate and direct wherever he wanted.

Maybe she was just more of a challenge. Yes. The Man would be drawn to a challenge.

Skull pulled his phone out of his pocket. He'd report what he saw to The Man and let him choose his own victim.

CHAPTER FIFTEEN
RYAN

———✸———

The neon OPEN sign was dark, but when I tugged on the front door of the Geneva Bar and Grill, it swung open. I let myself in.

"Hello! Weber?" My voice echoed off the concrete of the empty lobby. The red and green lanterns on either side of the counter sat cold and lifeless. I peeked through the wide doorway into the dining room. Chairs sat on top of tables, their legs sticking in the air. I couldn't help thinking of last week, when this place was packed during a Fourth-of-July rush. Thank God Jimmy's bomb hadn't gone off here, like he'd originally planned.

"Oh, hey!"

I turned at the voice. A large, round face appeared in the pickup window behind the front counter. Bud Weber held a metal spatula in one hand. The sounds of grilling wafted from the kitchen.

"How's it goin', Ryan?" he asked in his thick, Chicago accent.

It disgusted me that we were on a first-name basis. Given a dark alley and a lack of witnesses, there was no telling what we'd actually do to each other. "You got a

75

minute?" I asked. "Just wanted to go over some details again."

"Hell, yeah, I got a minute. Sure. Anything."

Weber's overly helpful manner disgusted me more than the grease on his spatula. I knew he was abusing Bailey. It wasn't a stretch for me to believe that he'd kidnapped, raped, and murdered Jimmy Beacon's sister, Amelia. We just couldn't prove any of it yet—beyond the fact that at the time of Amelia's disappearance from Racine, Weber had lived only ten minutes from her home. Yet all records pointed to his having a glittering past—all except the one I'd found this morning.

"Hey, you want somethun to eat?" Weber went on, his head still craned through the window. "It's on the house. Burgers? Soup? I've got beef Stroganoff ready in about ten minutes."

I held up a hand. "I'm good, thanks."

Weber stepped away from the window long enough to slot the spatula into a holder on his grill and wipe his hands on the dirty apron that covered his bulging middle. "How about a drink, then? Soda? Lemonade? Coffee? You want a beer? I'll never tell."

"No, thanks," I insisted again. "This shouldn't take long."

Weber wiped his hands some more. "Oh. Well, you wanna come back to the kitchen? I should keep an eye on my stove."

"Sure."

"Great." He flapped a hand through the pickup window. "Just help yourself to the soda fountain. Glasses are right there."

Ignoring his insistent hospitality, I made my way through the dining room and the dish room into the long, narrow kitchen. Over a glowing blue flame, Weber stirred a steaming pot of beef chunks and creamy gravy that smelled frustratingly good. Still, I wouldn't have been shocked if his kitchen was as full of roaches as his tongue was full of lies.

76

"Smells good," I commented. I had to be civil if I wanted any information out of him.

"Hey, thanks. Shit, grab yourself a plate." He motioned to the shelves above the grill, stacked with cream-colored ceramic ware.

I nodded at the stove. "You learned how to cook when you worked at Mama Neelah's?" I'd been doing my research on Weber. A lot more research. Mama Neelah's had been a hole-in-the-wall diner on the north side of Chicago, apparently a favorite in its own neighborhood.

Weber chuckled. "Shit, you been doing some homework. Yeah, I worked there. God, way back in high school. Started as a busboy. Made my way to waiter eventually. Then Mama Neelah figured I got a knack for cookin'. She put me in charge of baking the buns at first, and eventually I got to grill the steaks."

"And you dreamed of owning your own place ever since?"

"Sure, off and on. Never had the dough for it until, you know, five-six years ago when I opened up this place. Finally got a loan." He turned to me with a huge grin. "All bought and paid for now." He tossed down his spoon, laughing heartily.

I couldn't help thinking he paid that off fast.

Weber grabbed a massive kettle of noodles off another burner, hefted it to a nearby sink, and dumped the contents into a strainer. The rippled noodles steamed.

"Why Lake Geneva?" I asked. "Did you have ties here?"

He shrugged and shook the strainer, which rained water from the bottom. "Nah. Visited once or twice when I was a kid. But it's a tourist town, you know? If you can't make money here, you can't make money anywhere. Seemed like a smart place. And whatdya know? I was right. Business has been good." He poured noodles into a pair of stainless steel warming pans.

I glanced at the floor and scratched the back of my neck, dropping the next question casually. "Did Zayne Mars work at Mama Neelah's, too?"

I watched Weber's face like a hawk, though it was turned half away from me, shrouded in steam as noodles tumbled from his strainer into the pans. I thought a muscle twitched in his neck. That was all.

"Zayne? Hell, no. *I* didn't even work at Mama Neelah's anymore when I knew Zayne. Him and me had a little bitty apartment just off downtown. Roommates, you know? Drafty old place. Shit, we stuffed socks and underwear into the cracks in the brickwork. But the location was good. I was workin' at a fancy-ass restaurant, working my way up from the bottom all over again. And Zayne, he was into fashion and hair and makeup and God knows what. He was a strange bird, you know? Shit, he painted his fingernails. But hey, he forked over his rent on time. Anyway, he was saving up for his own place, too. Like a hair salon or somethun. Can't say I got any of it."

"Where were you when he was murdered?" I asked.

Bud didn't flinch. "Up in the apartment. Zayne went across the street to grab noodles for dinner. There was this little Thai place we kinda liked. Anyway, I hear *pop, pop, pop.*" He shrugged. "But it's Chicago, you know? Guns going off every night. Anyway, I have a peek out the window, and whatdya know? There's my roommate lyin' in the street, dead."

Bud's story matched perfectly with the reports I'd read that morning. Much as I wanted to peg him for a murder, I had no way of making this one stick. Not yet, at least.

"Why was Zayne killed?" I asked.

Bud shrugged. "What do they call it—a hate crime? He was off a bit, ya know what I'm sayin'? He liked guys. And some days, he didn't know if he was a dude or a chick." He humphed a laugh. "Queer bird. Still, I dunno why people

78

gotta stick themselves in other people's business. He paid his rent."

In the silence that followed, I struggled to wrap my mind around Bud's morals, but it hurt too much. He hurt girls—murdered them, maybe—but was upset that someone killed his queer roommate?

"That's when you moved to Racine," I observed. "After Mars died."

"Hell, yeah. I was sick of Chicago. Can't even eat noodles without somebody waving a gun in your face."

"I find it interesting you didn't mention any of this when we talked before," I said. We'd grilled Bud for hours after the bombing.

Bud lifted a spoonful of Stroganoff to his mouth and gave it a taste. "Why should I have?" He grabbed pepper off the counter and shook it generously over the kettle.

I shrugged. "We were talking about murder. Your roommate was murdered."

"We were talking about Jimmy and Amelia Beacon. It's not like they knew Zayne. I never thought of them in the same breath until you brought it up just now. Jesus Christ, you were askin' so many questions, how was I supposed to bring it up, anyway?" He gave the kettle a stir, then tapped the spoon on the side, flinging gravy back into the dish. "Look, hey, I'm sorry. Maybe I shoulda mentioned it. It was just such a long time ago, you know? And maybe it shook me up a bit, having a roommate killed, right out in my own street. Maybe I've tried not to think about it much. So yeah, sorry it didn't cross my mind to say somethin'." He shrugged and thrust his hands into oven mitts. "Well, you figured it out on your own anyway, so no loss in the long run." He hefted the Stroganoff onto a metal countertop and began ladling it into a new set of warming pans.

"Yeah," I agreed. "No loss in the long run." I still didn't get his morals.

Weber's nostrils flared as he concentrated on the dish he was preparing. "Look, hey, I'm all upset about Jimmy. He was a decent kid in his own way. Pretty good dishwasher. Showed up on time. He just had problems, you know? I've been thinkin' about him a lot, ever since he chased me all around with that bomb of his. I don't know how he got it into his head that I had anything to do with his little sis. He must have been crazy with grief, and it was just a pressure cooker, you know? It had to blow sometime." He glanced up quickly. "Oh, shit, sorry. Bad choice of words."

I waved it off, even though he was right for once. He was talking, and that's what I wanted.

"Anyhow, I'm just glad it wasn't worse. I'm real proud of Bailey for giving you folks a ring and warning you ahead of time. No telling how bad it could have been without you all on the scene—and shit, that police chaplain fellow. God, he was a real hero, throwin' himself over that bomb." He held up a hand. "I mean, sorry for your loss and all."

I didn't want his condolences for Bill Gallagher. Besides, my mind stuck on the words "proud of Bailey." No doubt he was proud of her every time she kept her mouth shut about the welts on her arms, the bruises around her eyes.

"We appreciate the sentiment," I lied. There was nothing I appreciated from Bud Weber, unless it were a confession. "Sorry to bring up bad memories. We just had to check into it."

"Yeah, sure, I get it." He held up a ladle full of stew. "Seriously, no Stroganoff?"

I raised a palm. "I'm good. Thanks anyway."

"Well, yeah. Any time. I mean it, too. I wanna help you guys. You know that, right?"

I merely nodded. "Thanks for your time, Bud."

I turned and walked out of the kitchen. That man made me want to barf. There were too many shady events swirling around both his past and his present. I just

80

couldn't get any of them to turn into something resembling probable cause.

But I swore he wouldn't escape me forever.

For Bailey's sake. I wasn't giving up on her.

CHAPTER SIXTEEN
BUD

———— ⚓ ————

As soon as the bell dinged over the door, Bud put a lid on his last warming pan, stuck it in the steam table, and made for his office. He closed the door behind him. Locked it. Reached up high on a shelf above his desk—the one where he kept his collection of beer steins. From the back, he pulled down one with a lid covered in dust. He hadn't touched it in years. But someone else had.

He plopped down into his desk chair and turned the stein over in his hands, examining the fingerprints that were too small to be his. This was, of course, where Jimmy Beacon had found the little pink bow with the butterfly on it. The one Amelia had been wearing the day she died. Finding that bow was what had started Jimmy on his rampage, convinced Bud had kidnapped and murdered little Amelia.

Bud had practically forgotten her name. But he'd never forget the way she cried that day he carried her off from the park in Racine. He'd put his hand over her mouth so no one would hear. Especially the scrawny half-wit of a kid that had been with her. Huh. Jimmy. Never thought their paths would cross again. He should be more careful about the people he hired.

No doubt, Ryan Brandt would have been interested to see this stein. But Bud had no intention of ever telling him about it or the things inside. Memories. Mementos. Bud lifted the lid. Jimmy had pawed through them all—the faux pearl necklace and earrings. The pocket knife.

While he was on the topic, there were other murders Bud Weber had never told the cops about.

Bud lifted the crusted tube of lipstick and the onyx locket with the silver spider on the lid. Zayne's.

His nostrils flared. This stein was private. Jimmy'd had no business digging around inside it like it meant nothing to anybody.

With a corner of his gravy-stained apron, Bud wiped the dust from the stein, and with it Jimmy's fingerprints. He'd stick the stein in his safe, along with the black leather vest he liked to wear when he was in a mood to kill. The cops never needed to find this.

Question was, what set Jimmy on to Bud in the first place? What led him to poke around in Bud's office and ultimately find his secret stash?

It didn't take no genius to figure it out. The Man was to blame for this. There were no two ways about it. He was still sore about that time Bud went rogue on his precious plan and shot Tommy Thomlin, the boat captain. Well, what was Bud supposed to do? Thomlin had been getting nosy, threatening to take Bailey away from him. He'd needed to teach Thomlin a lesson.

But in payment for messing up the plan, The Man Upstairs had sicced Jimmy and his bomb on Bud. Bud's spider senses and quick reflexes were the only things that had saved his bacon. The upshot? Jimmy was dead. Bud was alive. Jimmy's big plan had totally failed—and with it, The Man's.

Well, Bud had plans of his own now.

The Man was gonna pay for this.

CHAPTER SEVENTEEN
ANGELICA

———— ✸ ————

Roland Markham turned a page in the leather-bound photo album that rested on his lap. Angelica gasped, laying her finger on a faded picture. "He looks just like Kaydon!" Her older son took strongly after his father, with blond hair and blue eyes, leaving all his mother's Latina genes to his younger brother Mason.

Angelica and Roland sat knee-to-knee in a deep leather sofa in his study. Floor-to-ceiling bookshelves flanked the walls, an oceanic mahogany desk dominated the center of the room, and towering French doors gave a breathtaking view of the lake. This was the kind of house she loved to sell back in Malibu. The expensive ones. The dream homes. The castles. This place didn't look like it had been redecorated since its original design in the late nineteenth century, but it didn't need a thing changed. Every panel of wood and every converted gas lamp spoke of stately elegance and history.

Luxury like this hadn't existed in Angelica's tiny village in rural Mexico, where she butchered chickens in her own backyard and scrubbed the family laundry on a washboard. It had never so much as entered her wildest dreams until her family had left their village, crossed half of Mexico, and come to the States. She'd seen glorious architecture and stately buildings in Guadalajara, and on the other side of the border, she'd discovered the mansions overlooking the ocean. And now, as a realtor, these kinds of houses were literally her bread and butter. Historic, modern, rustic, tropic, she didn't care, so long as it had walk-in closets and a Jacuzzi. Once she had learned what luxury was, she had wanted it in every part of her life. Maybe it had even been part of her attraction to Will; he had money. Eventually, they had bought a gorgeous Spanish-style villa together in a gated community in Malibu.

Only now did she realize that mansions had been the staple of Will's life from birth, not something he had worked towards, like her. What on earth had led him to the disastrous decisions he made?

She tapped the photo. "How old is Will here?"

Roland leaned forward and placed his iced tea on a coaster on the coffee table. "Oh, eleven or twelve, I'd say."

Angelica smiled, bittersweet emotions mixing. "Kaydon is twelve."

This was the first she'd ever seen pictures of Will as a boy. It was a completely different story from the one he had fabricated about an abusive father and unhappy childhood. She could see now that the story had been a cover, a convenient way to never talk about his past. According to Roland, Paul and Kathleen Geissler had been loving parents, crushed by their son's betrayal, shunned by the community when the tale began to be told. They had sold their lake estate and returned to Chicago, where Roland still had occasional contact with them until their passing several years ago. Angelica was sad she would never meet her mother- and father-in-law. But there were still far too many emotions crashing through her system to fully dwell on that.

But between Roland's stories and these photos, the truth was slowly coming to light. Will's boyhood had been full of smiles and sunshine, sand and water and fireworks. The kind of privileged, carefree, innocent childhood she'd worked so hard to provide her own boys was the childhood her husband had lived.

Her boys. Carefree no longer. Not after losing their father. Not after beginning to glimpse the truth of who he was and what he had done. She couldn't shield them from it all, and she didn't want to. But she couldn't describe yet how they felt. What this had done to them. She was still a deer staring into the headlights herself. She should be more present for them. She would be, as soon as she got home. She would start over. She would have her answers—as many as she could find. If possible, she would leave knowing who had killed her husband and why. Then she could mourn properly. She would bury what needed to be buried, and she and her boys would find a way to move on.

Angelica stroked the photo of the pre-teen Will. "It must have killed him to leave this place," she said softly. "The memories. The magic."

There was no other word for it. The *magic* of this place. She looked through the French doors toward the lake itself, glittering, tranquil, eternal. She had come here expecting grit and blood, determined to find the reason behind it all. Instead, she had found a place that, until now, had known little but peace and goodwill. It hadn't taken long for the lake's quiet beauty to seep into her system. To whisper to her, suggesting that it, too, felt the pain of these recent days and the destruction that had come with them. It watched her, all-knowing, all-loving, a sentient, caring being as old as the earth. It wasn't quite real. The rain itself sparkled with sunshine.

She looked at Roland through vision gone blurry. "He was happy here, wasn't he?"

Roland nodded. "The happiest."

"Then..." Angelica blinked back tears. "How could he pretend it never happened?"

"He must have loved you and your sons very much to never speak of his past—to protect you from the man once known as Fritz Geissler. I've told you how his crimes destroyed his parents' reputation, as Bobby's nearly did mine. He was a man on the run. There was no way he could tell you the truth *and* have a life with you." He laid a hand on hers. "I hope you can believe that, Angelica. He did it to protect you."

She scowled and shook her head angrily. "You don't betray family," she said firmly.

"But for your own good. For your sons—"

She locked eyes with him. "Roland, there are many things I left behind in Mexico. Many friends and places and a thousand memories. When I crossed that border, I came with only one thing. *My family.* And that is the only thing I will ever have." She began to count items off on her fingers. "If my car breaks down, my papá will be there to fix it. If the furniture doesn't show up for a house staging, my mamá and my aunt will show up with furniture they got from God knows where. If I lose my husband—" her throat caught here. "My entire family will be there. Because that's what family is. They are *there* for you. You might be mad at them, you might shout at them, you might annoy each other to the moon and back. But at the end of the day, family is all you have. You *do not* betray your own family."

Roland regarded her carefully and nodded somberly. "That's why it's so very hard for you to accept how Will treated you."

Angry tears pricked her eyes. She tilted her head back, trying to keep them from falling, and breathed heavily. Studying the crown molding on the ceiling, she asked, "Were we even married at all?"

Roland reached for her hand and squeezed it tightly. "Nothing can negate the love you had for each other."

A single tear streamed down. "But who did I love?" She turned to face Roland again. "Was I in love with a dream? A made-up story? Someone who never existed?"

"He gave you his heart." He dipped his head, meeting her eye. "And I know—as well as you do—that his heart was gold."

His heart was gold... and yet he burglarized banks? He took other people's hard-earned money? Roland didn't understand. She brushed her tears away. There was no point dragging the conversation on when it was stuck in a dead end.

She turned again to the album and flipped a page. A black-and-white photo in the middle of the right-hand leaf caught her eye, clearly older than the rest. Yet like so many of the others, Geneva Lake was prominent in the background, easily identifiable by the white piers along the shore. Three young men, possibly in their twenties, smiled into the camera—but they were not Bobby, Fritz, and Jason.

Angelica squinted. "Roland, is that you?"

He slid the photo from the album, examining it through his readers, then turned it over. A date in a fine scrawl read 1959. He laughed. "Evidence of my terrible organizational skills. This belongs in a different album." He flipped it forward again and pointed. "An older set of musketeers. That's me, and that's Tommy Thomlin."

"Jason's father?"

"That's right."

She pointed to the third man, straight-backed and taller than Roland by a full head. "And who's this?"

Roland paused, lips slightly parted. His face seemed to sink. "That's Wade Erickson."

The name clashed through her head like a bell falling from a bell tower, hitting every stair on the way down. From her research, she knew this name well. "Wade Erickson?" she said, looking Roland in the eye. She squinted, unbelieving. "The man who killed your son?"

Roland nodded, still staring at the picture. He seemed to be lost in memory.

But for Angelica, the idea still didn't connect. It was unfathomable. "He was your friend?"

"The three of us were as close as Bobby, Fritz, and Jason ever were."

Angelica sank back into the sofa cushions, jaw slack. "One of your best friends... killed your son?"

Roland tossed the photo onto the coffee table as if casting it away from him. Groaning under his breath, he leaned back into the cushions. "We had fallen out long before that."

Angelica shook her head. "How?"

Roland stirred uncomfortably, hesitated, then heaved a rueful laugh. "As a teenager, Bobby developed a—well, a knack for trouble. Shoplifting. Breaking into candy machines." He shrugged. "Just little things. But after a while, I lost count how many times Wade drove him home in the back of his patrol car. Eventually, Wade became very firm with me." Roland sat up and scowled, as if imitating an angry Wade. "He told me if I didn't straighten my boy out, things would only grow worse." He shrugged. "Well, I didn't listen. I told Wade that Bobby was only sowing his wild oats and he'd grow out of it soon enough. It was practically a Markham family gene. I myself was a bit of a wild card when I was young."

Roland stared out the French doors overlooking the stone patio and the lake beyond. He twirled his thumbs. "But the next time it happened, Wade didn't drive Bobby home. He drove him to the police station and booked him. Put him in a cell. He had to appear before a juvenile court." Roland's brow went heavy as if confused. Betrayed. "The boy was only fourteen. I couldn't believe Wade did that." He sighed and turned up his palms. "Granted, I suppose Wade did the right thing. Bobby didn't get into any more trouble after that. Well, not until..."

His voice trailed off, leaving Angelica to fill in the rest. Not until he grew up and moved onto targets infinitely more sophisticated than candy machines.

Angelica frowned. Something didn't make sense to her. The other night, Roland had admitted that he blamed Will and Jason for leading Bobby astray. But how could he, when Bobby already had a history of petty criminal behavior at such an early age? Was Roland that blinded by fatherly devotion? Her own sons would be grounded for years if she ever caught them stealing.

On top of this, she couldn't help but wonder. Had Bobby truly quit his misbehavior after Wade taught him a lesson? Or had he simply gotten better? How did someone go from shoplifting candy bars as a boy to planning elaborate and wildly successful bank heists as an adult? Did he have help? If so, from whom?

Angelica rose from the sofa and paced between the sitting area and the desk, arms folded, chin in her hand, a lush Persian rug cushioning her steps. "Roland, who was there the night Bobby died?"

"Well... Fritz, Jason, Wade, and Wade's partner, Sidney Kruse. They were both detectives."

Angelica nodded. "Tell me what happened. Tell me the story the way you heard it. The way you were told."

Roland sighed and cast his eyes downward. Angelica had not given him a pleasant task, and she knew it. But she needed to know. He folded his hands around his knee and launched into the tale without further prompting.

"The boys had apparently been at it a few years and never were caught. Eventually, they got pretty brazen. For their next target—their last—they chose a bank right here in Lake Geneva, their hometown. They broke in, they loaded the contents of the vault into their getaway vehicle, they were about to leave, and—" Roland sighed heavily. "And that's when Wade and Sidney Kruse caught them in the alley behind the bank. Wade was a detective then. As I understand it, he'd taken an interest in the spate of bank burglaries that had taken place over several years across Chicago, Milwaukee, and Madison. They credit him as the first one to suppose they could all be connected." Roland shrugged. "I can't begin to imagine how he thought Bobby was behind them. A grudge he couldn't let go? It's beyond me."

Angelica moved to the French doors, framed by lush velvet drapes that piled on the floor. She stared across the lake. "Go on."

"Well, once again Wade was right. Who should come out of the bank, literally carrying the money bags, but Bobby, Jason, and Fritz?"

Here, Roland halted. Angelica knew why. She knew what had happened next. But this was the important part. The part she needed to know. "Please tell me," she muttered to the glass. "How did Bobby die?"

Silence lingered before Roland found his words. "Bobby was startled. He fired his gun." Roland stared at his hands again. "I can't imagine how frightened he must have been."

Angelica tuned out the excuses. They were inconsequential, if what she suspected was true. "So, Bobby shot first," she repeated. "According to whom?"

"Well... Wade, I suppose. Anyway, it was the conclusion of the grand jury. They ruled that Wade had fired in self-defense, and so there was no trial."

"Was there security footage?"

"No. If I remember, the boys disabled all the cameras."

Angelica nodded. How convenient. "Police dash cams?"

"I believe their unmarked car wasn't outfitted with a camera."

She smirked. Also convenient. "What happened to Wade's partner? Sidney Kruse?"

"He caught a bullet. Died at the scene."

"Whose bullet? Who killed him?"

"Jason."

92

"Based on Wade's testimony?"

"Yes, I suppose so. I imagine there was some forensic evidence backing that up, as well. The location of shell casings, or however that works."

Angelica chewed on her lip. Jason killed the only other witness? That didn't fit her developing theory. But she could think of explanations. Maybe Jason was in on it. Maybe the police lied about the evidence. "And Jason and Will vanished," she concluded the story. "Disappeared without a trace. Were never heard from again until now."

"That's right."

Angelica turned and met his gaze. "In other words, five men entered the alley that night. And only *one* remained to tell the tale?"

"Well, yes. But as I said, the forensics—"

Angelica blew through her lips and waved her hand. "Evidence can be staged. At the end of the day, Wade Erickson got to tell his story *his* way, and there was no one else to say otherwise, not even his partner."

Roland frowned and tilted his head suspiciously. "What are you suggesting?"

"The fourth member of the Markham Ring. What if we knew who he was all along?"

Roland tilted his head. *"Wade?"*

"Yes."

Roland fell back into the cushions, frowning, turning over the idea, not looking particularly convinced.

Angelica held up a finger. "Listen. Bobby gets himself arrested when he's fourteen, and then he never breaks the law again. But did he have a change of heart, or did he have *help?* Maybe Wade found a reason to turn a blind eye. Maybe he taught Bobby how to hit bigger and bigger targets. Maybe he cleaned up after Bobby—for a price. For a cut of the profits."

Roland opened his mouth, but no words came out.

It didn't matter. Angelica was on a roll. She began to pace. "It's years later. Bobby's all grown up, and he's playing in the big leagues. He's taking down banks. But he needs help, and that's why he recruited Will and Jason—however he talked them into it." She rolled her eyes dramatically. "And the newspapers say, 'Oh, Wade Erickson, he was the first one to link all these burglary cases.'" She threw up her hands. "Really? Chicago's not his jurisdiction. Milwaukee's not his jurisdiction. *Lake Geneva* is—this tiny little town that has nothing to do with them. He wasn't linking cases; he was *in* on them."

She tapped her chin with the nail of her manicured thumb. Was she a lunatic, or had she hit on something? "Are we supposed to believe the Markham Ring just *happened* to choose Lake Geneva next, the town where this one little detective was piecing things together, linking these intricate heists to the boy who used to help himself to candy bars? Do you realize how crazy that even sounds? How much money could they even expect to take from a bank in a town this small? And the next thing you know, Bobby and Sidney Kruse are both dead, Jason and Will have vanished, and Wade Erickson is free to sing whatever song he wants. And here's the only thing we need to know." She pointed a finger across the room at Roland. "Did Bobby shoot first—or was it Wade?"

Her words hung in the air. Roland didn't so much as blink, much less offer a rebuttal. At last, he stirred. "But... why? If Wade was in fact benefiting from Bobby's activities, why would he kill him? That's turning off the faucet, don't you think?"

Angelica shrugged. "Relationships go sour. People get greedy. Maybe Bobby was short-changing Wade. Or getting careless and becoming too much of a liability. There could be dozens of reasons."

Roland leaned back, silent, and Angelica knew she was making her case. "But… he's always lived simply, not like a man of means…"

She tilted her head. "If you were chief of police over a small department, would you live like you had millions? Maybe he's got a bank overseas. Or he's going to retire in style abroad. Maybe he's got a second wife somewhere. Maybe he's just a hoarder."

Roland shook his head. "I just can't believe…"

Angelica planted a hand on her hip. "Why not?"

"Well, I've known him since he was this tall." Roland held his hand two and a half feet off the floor. "We called him 'Shorty' because he didn't hit his growth spurt until he was fifteen. I played baseball with him when we were kids." He shook his head, turning his hands palms-up. "He was a brother to us, Tommy and me. We looked out for him."

Angelica folded her arms and couldn't help looking at him pityingly. Bobby couldn't be a bad boy, because he was Roland's son—even though Roland admitted Bobby had committed petty crimes as a teen. And Wade Erickson couldn't be guilty, because he had been Roland's friend—even though the two of them had fallen out years ago.

"Roland, you are the blindest man I have ever met."

He dropped his gaze without arguing and twirled his thumbs, looking more humbled than affronted.

Angelica sighed and fell into the sofa beside him, lacing her fingers around her own knee, imitating his stance. For several moments, they gazed across the room and the lake and said nothing.

Roland was the one to break the silence. "Do you think he killed your husband?"

Angelica let the question soak in. Let it seep in through her pores, enter her bloodstream, and become part of every fiber of her being. Of all the questions she had come here to answer, this one was at the center of it all. Who had killed her husband? Why now, after all these years? Where was the culprit? Why was he still free? Why was someone allowed to devastate her life like this—stealing not only the love of her life, but every precious memory she had of him? She reviewed everything she now knew—the facts of the case. And everything she now suspected. And then she closed her eyes and tuned in to her heart.

"I don't know," she said. "I need evidence."

Roland nodded. In the distance, power boats cut the lake. "I'll help you, if I can."

Angelica smiled and took his hand. She wasn't sure where she'd be if she hadn't met Roland.

The stately grandfather clock against the wall groaned to life and struck the hour.

CHAPTER EIGHTEEN
ANGELICA

———✸———

Angelica peered through a glassed-in service window toward the collection of desks and office chairs beyond, two of which were currently staffed. She'd never requested trial transcripts at a courthouse before, so she wasn't sure what to expect. Hopefully, this wouldn't take long.

A woman glanced up, noticed Angelica, and rose from her desk. She approached the window.

"Can I help you?" Her voice emanated from a circular speaker mounted in the glass. Her short, wavy blond hair had gone gray at the roots, and she apparently hadn't learned how to let her makeup enhance her features instead of painting them over. Still, her eyes were kindly, and Angelica wasn't here to give style tutorials.

"Hello," she said. "I'd like to request the records on a court proceeding?"

The woman nodded. "Let me get you a request form."

A request form? Forms took time to process. Angelica had the sinking feeling she might not receive her documents this afternoon, as she'd hoped. Still, she would go through with it. It would be worth the wait. "Thank you."

The clerk walked to a file cabinet.

Angelica toyed with her clutch. She knew from the newspapers that a jury had declared Wade not guilty of murder. The transcript would contain every iota of evidence that had been collected that night. She needed to review it. To search for a flaw. Roland had told her to ask at the county courthouse in Elkhorn, only a ten-minute drive from the lake. And so here she was.

The clerk pulled a slip of paper from the file cabinet, then returned to the window. Laying it on the desk on her side of the glass, she pointed out two separate sections.

"Just fill out this part here, and leave this one blank."

Angelica nodded. The woman slid the paper through the tray under the glass, along with a pen. Angelica thanked her, then found a nearby chair to sit and write.

The form requested the date, time, and location of the incident in question, and the name of an involved person. For the name, she put in Wade Erickson, feeling a little nervous about leaving a paper trail indicating she was investigating the case. For the type of proceeding, she wrote "grand jury transcript, reports, etc."

At the bottom, she noted a charge of fifty cents per page, which was no problem. But there was also a note explaining that a records request would require ten business days for a response. She sighed, but checked the box asking to have the documents mailed to her at her address in Malibu. She'd be home again by that time.

She stood and approached the window again. The clerk met her on the other side, and Angelica slid her paper through. The woman scanned it.

"Oh, honey, I'm sorry. We can't release these records."

Angelica's heart skipped a beat. "I'm sorry?"

The woman turned the page so Angelica could see it and pointed out the line where she had written, "grand jury."

"Grand jury proceedings are secret."

Angelica frowned. "Secret? I thought all court proceedings were public record."

"Not grand juries, dear. A grand jury convenes to determine whether to indict a person of felony offenses—whether to bring them to trial. The proceedings are secret to protect the witnesses and the jury against retribution."

Angelica felt as if something had been stolen away from her. Hope. Facts. *Truth.* "And if the grand jury did not indict someone, there would be no trial—and thus no trial records and transcripts?"

"That's correct."

Angelica's heart sank. The grand jury had indeed failed to indict Wade Erickson. He had never been accused of murder, and never stood trial. Without the records from the grand jury, where else could she find details?

"Is there nothing that would be public record?" she asked, desperate. "Surely they at least published their findings? Their conclusions? A report of some sort?"

"I can look," the woman offered, giving a kind smile.

"That would be very meaningful to me."

The woman took a pen and added a note. "If nothing was released to the public, I'll send you a note anyway."

Angelica's heart filled with gratitude. "Thank you so much. I appreciate the extra work you'll go through."

"It's no problem, dear. Is there anything else I can help you with?"

"No. Thank you."

They said their good-byes and Angelica headed back to her car, her high hopes a wreck. But she squared her shoulders. There had to be other options. Other records and documentation detailing what happened that night.

She would go to the source, if she had to.

CHAPTER NINETEEN
MONICA

———⚓———

The light had long since faded outside the windows of the detective bureau. My partners and I were working overtime again. I was finally typing up the report from our visit to the Abbey Resort.

Lehman and I had been lucky enough to talk with the clerk who had served Fritz Geissler at the front desk. Geissler hadn't had a reservation. He'd walked in around one in the morning on June sixteenth. He'd been polite, but his demeanor was forced. The clerk felt as if Geissler had really been tired and stressed, as if he were pissed off about something. He only stayed the one night. He never asked for room service. He had no visitors. In fact, he only stayed at the hotel a few hours. He checked out at 4:45 a.m.

According to the medical examiner, Geissler had been murdered no later than 7:00 a.m. that same morning.

Lucky for us, Geissler's hotel room was empty today. Unfortunately, it had been cleaned—more than once, in fact. We searched anyway. And of course, we found nothing.

We knew that Geissler's plane from LA to Chicago had landed at 9:05 p.m. on the fifteenth. Which meant, if he'd driven straight to Geneva Lake, a ninety-minute commute, he'd spent a grand total of, at most, eight and a half hours in the area before he died. Subtracting the four hours he spent at the Abbey, we had to account for just four and a half hours of his life, maybe less. Four and a half hours that led to his murder.

Meanwhile, our evidence files now contained a copy of the death certificate for someone named William Michael Read from Grand Rapids, Michigan—in other words, Fritz's alias. The real Will Read had died in 1997—the same year Fritz disappeared. I wondered if Fritz had been skilled in forging IDs as well, or if he'd had help stealing Mr. Read's identity.

Tonight, there were still far more questions than answers.

Lehman sighed and clicked his mouse loudly—the sign that he was finally putting his computer to sleep. I heard his voice beyond the gray cubicle wall. "Whatdya think, Neumiller? Call it a day?"

Mark Neumiller groaned appreciatively. "Don't have to ask me twice."

Lehman's chair squeaked as he stood, his head and shoulders appearing above the divider. He gripped his hands together overhead and arched his back. "Anybody down for a beer? My ex has the kids, and the cat isn't talking to me 'cause I forgot the canned food."

"You're on," Neumiller agreed, tossing files into a cabinet and turning the key in the lock.

Lehman leaned over the top of the cubicle, staring down at me. "Steele?"

"Another time," I replied. "I have a few things to finish up."

"It's okay to breathe for a minute." He nodded, as if berating himself for saying something asinine. "Oh, I forgot. You *don't* know that." He tried a new tactic. "What if I buy?"

"Rain check," I said, still typing. All I wanted was for him and Neumiller to go away.

101

Neumiller slung his jacket over his shoulder and shrugged. "You tried, Lehman. She has a date with her job."

Lehman cocked an eyebrow at me. "Well, I expect a wedding invitation when you two finally tie the knot."

I shifted an eyebrow at him. "Noted."

The guys turned and left, chatting on their way out. Their demeanor was subdued, not like they were about to hit the bars. This case had us all exhausted and constantly on our toes. What if, while we finally took a rest at the end of the day, The Man Upstairs made another move? What if, while we sifted through details, he moved mountains, ruining more lives? We never felt safe.

Still, Lehman had a point. Working myself to exhaustion ran the risk of dulling my mind.

Especially if I was secretly working two cases at once.

For the next half hour, above the clack of my own keys, I listened to the sounds outside my door, waiting until the station felt sleepy—or at least as sleepy as a police station ever gets.

When I was convinced the last of the day-shifters were gone, I picked up my cell phone and searched my contacts. Tara Slater. We hadn't talked in years.

I took a deep breath and hit send. The phone rang. Tara's voice came over the line.

"Well, hey, stranger! Long time, no chat."

I smiled. She was the kind of friend you could pick up with right where you left off. I leaned back in my desk chair and swiveled lazily, letting the movement dissipate my anxiety. "Hey, Tara. What up in Madtown?"

"Oh, the yoozh. We added a new position in homicide. You looking for a job? We miss you up here."

I grinned, a touch of nostalgia creeping in. Tara and I had shared an office in the Madison PD Detective Bureau. Lunch breaks usually found us at any one of the small ethnic restaurants on State Street—Thai, Greek, Russian, Indian, take your pick—or at a coffee shop that served beet sandwiches and offered water in upcycled glass jars. On weekends, we jogged together on the shore of Lake Mendota, winding our way past the stately, historic buildings of the University of Wisconsin-Madison. And like any self-respecting Madisonian, we proudly wore tee shirts sporting pink plastic flamingos.

But for all the fond memories, you'd have to threaten me at gunpoint to get me to go back. Madison was the city where my marriage had fallen apart. Where Ryan had had a fling with another woman. Madison was where I'd finally gotten pregnant. And where I'd had my abortion.

I diverted the conversation away from the notion of returning. "I'll wager Lake Geneva is more exciting than Madison right now."

"No shit, lady. I get the news from Luke." Luke Foreman from Madison PD Homicide had volunteered to join the investigative task force. He made the ninety-minute drive three times a week to attend our morning meetings. "What the hell's going on over there?" Tara demanded.

"Well, that's the question, I guess."

Tara's voice turned serious and sincere. "What do you need from me, girl?"

I twirled a pen on my desk, my stomach cramping. Tara Slater was deeply intuitive. It didn't shock me that she already knew this wasn't a social call.

"I just need to know..." My mouth went dry. Aside from the staff at the clinic that performed my abortion, Tara was the only person who knew about my pregnancy. I'd had to tell *someone.* And with her whole heart, Tara had offered me a shoulder to cry on. She helped me think through all the options—even though I'd been in no thinking mood. As always, I'd wanted swift and sudden action. But when I chose, she didn't judge. She offered to go to my appointment with me. In the end, I took that journey alone. But I had never forgotten her willingness and support.

103

And then we never spoke of it again. She knew it was off limits. But sometimes a spark of knowing passed between our eyes. And hers always seemed to say, *I'm here for you. I'm ready to talk when you are.*

But I'd brushed that offer off as well, telling myself I was fine.

Now, ten years later, how did I bring it up again? How did I ask her... whether she had really kept my secret?

"I just need to know..." I tried again. "Tara, did you ever tell anyone about...?"

She seemed to know immediately what I was trying to get at. "No. Never. Not even Max." Her husband.

The fear released my heart, one piercing claw withdrawing at a time. I found myself sniffing back a tear. "Thanks," I said in a husky voice. "That means a lot to me." And it did. But if Tara had never told, how did The Man Upstairs seem to know about my pregnancy? Or was I interpreting his words incorrectly? But if he wasn't talking about my baby, what *was* he talking about? *Yes, Monica, YOUR children...*

"Why do you ask?" Tara inquired. She gave a little gasp. "Ryan hasn't found out, has he?"

"No, no, he hasn't."

"Oh, thank God. That would be... awkward." The word itself fell short, and she knew it.

I leaned forward to place an elbow on my desk, cupping my whole upper body around my phone. "It's... it's related to the case we're working on."

"What do you mean?"

I closed my eyes for a moment, the voice of The Man Upstairs circling through my head. "We're trying to locate a suspect. A suspect who..." His words stabbed into my heart again. "Tara, I think he knows."

"What?"

Forcing my emotions to remain at bay, I told her about the phone call I'd received moments after the bombing. The

104

challenge to play The Man's game. The boast that he knew everything about everyone in town—even me. The hint that maybe—maybe—he knew about my child.

"Holy shit," Tara breathed. "Monica, I promise, I never said a word."

"I know. I believe you."

"That leaves only one option."

"The clinic."

"Someone who worked there?"

"It has to be."

"Do you want me to look into it?"

I thought about that. "No." I was already out of bounds, sharing details of the case with someone who wasn't assigned to it. Right now, the only person outside of the task force who knew about that phone call was The Man Upstairs. If we caught a suspect and he let on that he knew about the call, we'd know we had our man. It was bad enough that I'd shared this detail with Tara. It could only make things worse if I let her involve herself in my investigation. "I'll look into it myself," I said.

"Okay." She seemed to think for a moment. "Have you told the task force?"

I drew circles on my desk with the back end of a pen. "No."

She didn't answer. Her way of not judging, but silently forcing me to consider what I was doing.

"Ryan's on the task force." It was all I needed to say.

"Ah."

Silence stretched uncomfortably. I knew what she was going to say before she said it.

"Have you considered telling him?"

I bit my lips together. Under different circumstances, maybe I would have. Or rather, I would have let him find out. I pictured Ryan walking into the meeting room just as Lehman added a note to the marker board in bright red ink: *Monica's baby.* Ryan's reaction would be the same as if

105

someone had put a slug between his eyes. To hold a secret this long, only to dish it up semi-publicly for the sake of an investigation, would be the ultimate way to let him know how much I hated him.

Except that I didn't hate him anymore.

Quite possibly I was in love with him.

I was nowhere near being able to explain any of that to Tara. I hadn't squared with it myself yet. Nor had I figured out how I could possibly tell Ryan about our child more privately. Not without losing him all together. My only excuse was that I couldn't bear to raise our child alone—to see a miniature version of Ryan's face every day, reminding me both of him and of what he had done to me. To us. All three of us.

Had I considered telling Ryan? Yes. A thousand times, in a thousand different ways. None of them seemed right—or even like the right thing to do.

"That's not an option," I said, and left it at that.

"You sure?"

I thought again of the shock that would pass through his eyes, followed by the anger. I wasn't able to face that yet. "Yes."

"Okay." She was quiet for a moment. "You're investigating this on your own?"

"Yes."

I waited, maybe hoping she'd shrive my soul. God knew, I should have told the task force. I was playing with fire, not sharing everything I knew. What if I hamstrung the investigation? What if running an independent inquiry put me or my colleagues in danger? I was a cop who played by the strictest interpretation of the rules. Always. No exceptions.

Until now.

I guess we each have our own breaking point. I had clearly reached mine. My psyche was a mess.

But once again, Tara neither condoned nor condemned my actions. Perhaps it was merely a way of shriving her own soul of my questionable decisions. "You're walking a wire," was all she said. An observation, and nothing more.

I dipped my head, as if I had to hide my shame over the phone. "I know."

"What are you going to do if you turn up anything?"

"I'm not sure. I'll find a way to get the relevant details to the task force."

"But not your pregnancy?"

"I'll cross that bridge when I come to it."

Tara sighed. "Okay. Well... you know I'm here for you."

I smiled "Thanks. I appreciate that."

We said good-bye and hung up. I folded my arms on my desk and dropped my head on top of them. Damn The Man Upstairs. Who was he? How did he know? I had to find him. And I had to find him first—before the task force did. The truth would be out as soon as he was caught. And every word he said would be hashed over a thousand times.

I even know how to exploit your children. Yes, Monica— YOUR children.

What did you mean by those words? some interrogator would ask.

And he would tell them. And my life as I knew it, both good and bad, would be over.

The Man Upstairs had invited me to play his game. But maybe he had already won. He'd told me his goals: Control. Manipulation. Clearly, he already had perfect control over me. In some dark room hidden from my sight, he was chuckling to himself. Reveling in my mental turmoil. If he really knew everything, then he knew that I was a crumpled wreck. Fighting to protect my secrets. Fighting to find him. And shedding fresh tears for the baby I'd wanted desperately, then didn't keep because I didn't know how to be anything short of an asshole.

With the whisper of a few words in my ear, The Man Upstairs completely owned me.

CHAPTER TWENTY
RYAN

———✵———

Once the elevator doors had parted, I stepped out onto the second floor of the police station and looked down the hall toward the detective bureau. It was late, and I had a hunch that Monica, never sensible about little pleasantries like sleeping and eating, would still be there. I hoped she was. I needed to apologize for not being the one to tell her that I was staying with the LGPD.

A door clicked behind me. I turned to see who it was and found Chief Wade Erickson leaving the executive suite, where he and the lieutenant had their offices.

I paused as he made his way toward the elevator and hooked a thumb on my duty belt. "Calling it a day, chief?" I asked.

"Yep. Nancy told me she'd throw the rest of the lasagna in the trash if I didn't get home soon."

I laughed. Then remembered Wade and Nancy had special company at their house. "Hey, how's Tommy?" I hadn't seen him in weeks.

Wade shrugged. "Grumpy. Impatient. Basically back to normal, in other words." He laughed.

I smiled. "Glad to hear that. Hey, I don't suppose Bailey Johnson's dropped in to visit, has she?" The last time I'd spoken to her was the day of the bombing, when she'd called to tip me off to Jimmy Beacon's intentions. For a while before that, I'd brought her to the hospital every day. It had seemed to mean a lot to her to be near Tommy, even if his speech was incoherent for days. I had held out hope that, between me and the captain, we could finally unlock her soul—maybe get her to admit that Bud Weber was abusing her. But as soon as Tommy woke up, she had abruptly terminated the visits. All my calls and texts after that had gone unanswered. I still had no idea what had gone wrong.

Wade shook his head. "I haven't seen her."

I chewed my cheek. "I'll check on her." She'd only broken the silence that once to warn me about Jimmy. I wasn't the one who interviewed her afterwards. I was busy getting stitches for a ball bearing that nearly took out my noggin.

"While you're at it," said the Chief, "see if she knows anything about Weber's previous lives." He leaned in closer and lowered his voice, as if to prevent Weber himself from hearing. "Maybe talk to social services. See if there's any way to get her into a different home. The longer she's with Weber, the less I like it."

I nodded somberly. I couldn't agree more. In fact, I'd already done some research—and it wasn't promising. According to state law, Weber could only be denied his foster home license if he were *convicted* of a crime. Still, I couldn't help but think that social services would try to pull some strings for us, once they understood the kinds of offenses for which he was under investigation.

Wade checked his watch. "I'd better run before that lasagna hits the trash."

I nodded. "Have a good night, Chief."

The elevator bell dinged, and Wade stepped through the doors. A moment later, he was gone.

I puffed my cheeks, then turned my attention once again to the door to the Detective Bureau. Time to face the tiger. I continued down the hall and stopped to peek through the narrow glass pane. The lights were on, but the desks were empty—except for one. Monica stared into her monitor as if her scowl could force it to relinquish the answers she sought.

I couldn't help but smile. No other woman had ever been that beautiful in my eyes. The tidy ribbon of her mahogany hair trailed down her back. Her brown eyes, almost black, were intense as storm clouds. Every feature of her face remained sharp and focused like an icebreaker, forcing immovable objects to shatter before her path.

There was much she kept close to her vest. I wanted to know it all. But if there was anything I had learned from Bill Gallagher, it was to respect her space—to simply stand by to support her. If she so chose, maybe one day she would trust me with the burdens of her heart.

And that trust started with my coming clean. Apologizing for not telling her right away that she was stuck with me—unless she decided to keep her promise and dump all our asses.

Butterflies in my chest, I pushed open the door.

CHAPTER TWENTY-ONE
MONICA

———— ⎈ ————

Mesmerized, I listened to the voice as it hissed over my speakers.

"I know your strengths. I know your weaknesses..."

My ears were on The Man; my eyes were on my phone. *Call me, I dare you. Give me another clue. I WILL find you.*

I should have been researching names related to the clinic where I had my abortion. Instead, I'd been drawn back to the recording like a moth to flame. The chilling message rasped to the end. I dragged the slider bar back to the beginning and listened over. Who was he? Did I know him? Even if he'd disguised his voice, was there anything I could recognize?

Call me...

"A frown like that might crack your screen."

I started and looked up. "Ryan." He stood just inside the doorway, arms folded, a teasing smile on his lips. I fumbled with my mouse, trying to hit the pause button. *"Yes, Monica—YOUR chil—"* I finally connected with the button and stopped the unearthly voice, my heart pounding.

Ryan's smile turned into a concerned frown. He stepped further into the room and motioned toward my computer. "What the hell was he talking about, anyway?"

"Nothing," I said, then realized I'd said it too quickly. Ryan quirked his head, lifting an eyebrow. "He's psycho," I added. "I mean..." I shrugged and snorted, waving a dismissive hand at the screen. "He thinks he's God."

Ryan laughed through his nose. "Yeah." He leaned against a table opposite my desk. I'd gotten used to him in cargo shorts and a shirt with a royal blue blaze across the shoulders—the bike patrol uniform. Tonight, he was dressed head-to-toe in the navy blue of a regular patrolman. He jabbed his chin at my computer. "I thought County was working on the audio?"

I shrugged and minimized the file. "Yeah, well, you know me. Gotta do my own work plus everybody else's."

He nodded, smiling again. "Oh yeah, that's right." He looked at me sincerely. "I hope you're not letting him get to you."

I dropped my gaze and twiddled a pen. Let an edge creep into my voice. "You know me," I repeated.

Ryan nodded. He understood. And he wouldn't get in my way. "I dropped in because..." He jabbed his head in the general direction of the conference room. "I didn't mean for you to find out that way. I meant to tell you myself. Wade asked me to fill Schultz's position. I said yes. But you should have heard that from me."

I quirked a snarky smile. "You didn't tell me you were seeing another woman, either." I meant his affair in Madison. But why was I always looking to shoot him down? To keep him at arm's length?

"I will apologize for that as many times as you need."

I lifted an eyebrow. His response was kind of... chivalrous. And yet his back was straight, his head held tall. He wasn't demeaning himself. He was a man who had come to terms with the suckiness of his past self—but no longer living with it. At the very least, he had its back against the wall.

He bowed his head and scratched his neck. "I, uh... I'm not trying to crowd you out. I hope you know that."

My jaw clenched. Truth be told... I was really confused right now. I had been ever since the bomb went off and Ryan threw himself over me, offering his own body to shield mine.

No, before that. When we both jumped up on that park bench, drawing our sidearms in sync, like two bodies with one mind. Together, we tried to take down Jimmy Beacon before he could pull the detonator cord and devastate our town. Knowing that if we succeeded, we would devastate our own minds—because who could live with killing a sixteen-year-old boy? Believing, like we did once upon a time, that maybe we'd be there for each other to clean up the mental mess. To cry. To scream. To pound the wall. To hold each other close and let the tremors pass. Had we? No. Would we?

I didn't know.

For weeks, we'd circled each other, me growling, him cowering. But at first opportunity, our rhythms had fallen into sync. One soul. One mind. One purpose. We once had believed that there was nothing we couldn't overcome together.

I leaned back in my chair, mulling his unspoken question of whether I was leaving. "I mean, I'd have to be some kind of asshole to peace out in the middle of an investigation like this."

A smile turned up the corner of his mouth. His eyes twinkled. My staying made him happy.

It made *me* happy. I should have hated myself for that. Instead, I worried that the conversation was over. That Ryan would leave. I didn't want him to leave.

I wanted to bury my face in his chest and cry. I wanted to feel him comfort me the way he used to. I wanted to stop being the only one carrying my mental mess.

Ryan waved at my computer. "Anything I can help you with? Get you out of here a little faster tonight?"

I eyed the icon representing the media file player. I didn't want his comfort so much that I would risk letting him get near my investigation of The Man Upstairs. I tried to wrap my mind around telling Ryan about my abortion—and once again, my brain took a hard left. He was a different man. His fathering instinct had finally kicked in. He was sorry for ruining our marriage. There was no way he could love me, knowing what I'd done without his knowledge or consent.

I shook my head. "I'm leaving soon anyway."

He nodded. "Okay." Then he took in a breath and clapped his hands on his thighs. "Well. Now that I'm staying, I guess I should finally unpack."

I raised an eyebrow. "You haven't unpacked?"

He shrugged again. "I mean, the boxes make such a great dining table."

A laugh snorted its way past my defenses.

He smiled. A smile I hadn't seen in more than ten years. There was light in his eyes. Life. Heat. Interest.

He was absolutely in love with me. He proved it with his next words.

He gestured towards my desk again. "If you ever need a break from all this..." He fumbled towards what he was trying to say. "I can nuke a really good frozen dinner."

Against my better judgment, I laughed again. So I turned away and swiveled my chair. What was I doing? I shouldn't encourage him. But the concrete wall between me and the world was fissuring. The warmth was creeping in. Calling to me. Begging me to give it a chance. Taking a breath, I mentally cracked the door open. I didn't know why. Just to flirt with the dangers that lived outside.

115

Possibilities slipped in like a stray cat. So bruised and unloved. But with so much potential.

But when I tried to open that door any wider, all I felt was emptiness inside. A jumble of ugly secrets cluttered the path. Twisted my soul. Stole the words away. My eye drifted to the media file.

Yes, Monica, YOUR children...

"I'll keep it in mind," I said, my smile crashing. The fear building.

Ryan nodded. "No worries." The excitement faded from his eyes, but he looked neither crushed nor surprised. He pushed off from the table. "Need anything, give me a call."

I nodded but couldn't draw out another word, or so much as look at him. He walked out, closing the door softly. Silence settled in behind him. The very walls seemed to watch me, silent, sad, disappointed. Like a thousand nights, I was alone in the office, nothing to keep me company but a glowing screen and the profiles of a hundred criminals.

Tonight, my companion was The Man Upstairs.

I was lousy at choosing who I hung out with.

TUESDAY
JULY 15, 2014

CHAPTER TWENTY-TWO
RYAN

———— ⚓ ————

I leaned against a brick half-wall, enjoying the shade of the Riviera breezeways, the view of the lake, and a ham sandwich from Potbelly's down the street. I figured I may as well take my lunch here and catch Bailey as she came off work.

Meanwhile, my thoughts constantly returned to last night. My stomach filled with butterflies, which made no sense. Monica had declined my lousy idea of date night—as well she should. But she had smiled. She had laughed. I felt as giddy as I had in high school when I first realized we were more than "just friends."

A whistle blew. Moments later, the Mailboat eased around the end of the pier and nosed toward its berth. I smiled when I saw Bailey standing on the rub board at the bow of the boat, a coiled rope in her hand. She looked up and spotted me. I lifted my sandwich in a wave. She gave me a little wave back. The boat slid parallel to the pier, and she hopped off to tie her line. When she was done, she turned to me and lifted a finger.

I nodded. I was in no rush, unless my radio squawked. I remembered her routine from my own days as a mail jumper: Moor the boat, drop the gangway in place, disembark the passengers (probably pose for a few photos), then tidy the boat quick for the next round of tourists.

I watched her chat with the happy excursionists. One of them, an elderly lady, pinched Bailey's cheek, and from my post ten yards away, I heard her call Bailey "so gosh-darn cute." Bailey smiled. If she was offended, she didn't show it. But she was good at looking cheerful, regardless of whatever emotions were going on inside. So, I felt offended for her. That woman had no idea that, for Bailey, human touch meant bruises more often than not. Much as I wanted to wrap that girl in a protective hug, I knew it was off the table until Bailey herself allowed it.

The passengers gone, Bailey exchanged a word with the second mail jumper, motioning to me. The other jumper, a blond-haired boy, nodded and entered the boat, where I saw him sort boxes of mail.

Bailey walked up the pier toward me. The lake breeze played with her ponytail, and she brushed fly-aways out of her face. Dressed in white shorts and a navy-blue tee shirt, she was the embodiment of summer in Lake Geneva. It was hard to think of the shadows that dogged her.

She pulled herself up onto the half-wall beside me. I held out my open bag of sour cream and onion potato chips, and when she cupped her palms, I poured some in. She popped one into her mouth and joined me in staring over the lake, as if our sharing a lunch were the most natural thing in the world. I guess you could say we knew each other by now.

"This is where we exchange the secret info, right?" she quipped.

"Yup." I tried to keep a straight face and failed. I wanted to forget that I actually *had* come here to gather some info. "Sorry I haven't seen you. They put me on a task force on top of my patrol duties. I've been busy."

She shrugged. It was no biggie to her. But I couldn't forget the challenge that Bill Gallagher had dumped at my feet before he died: Relentless love. A love that never abandoned someone, especially when they'd already been abandoned so many times. Bailey was in her fourteenth foster placement.

It suddenly dawned on me that the change in my job status might actually be meaningful to her.

"By the way, I don't know if you even knew this," I started, "but until last week I was just a reserve officer."

She crinkled her nose. "Reserve officer?" She ate another chip.

"Yeah. A temporary officer. I was only supposed to be here for the summer."

She popped her eyebrows. "Oh." The information was new to her, but not earth-shattering. "'Was'?"

"Yeah. They took me on permanent."

She stared across the lake, her eyes distant, as if her mind were turning. "Because that other cop died."

For a moment, I was knocked speechless. I'd forgotten how perceptive she could be. Her silence hid much. "Yes. Because the other cop died."

She nodded, turning a chip in her fingers. "So... you're staying?"

I nodded. "I'm staying."

Her brow flinched in thought. "Cool." And that was all she said. If my words meant anything at all to her, it was unreadable.

"How are you doing with Jimmy's death?"

She looked down and shrugged. "It's weird. His not being around. He had a crush on me, you know?"

I nodded, letting her go on.

"And sometimes I think... I don't know. Maybe if I wasn't so hard on him...?"

I saw the lost look on her face. The hopelessness. The second-guessing. I caught her eye. "Hey, Jimmy's death is not your fault, okay? There were a lot of issues he was dealing with. Most of them had nothing to do with you."

She dropped her head and nodded. I could only hope some part of what I said would stick. I couldn't stand to think she blamed herself for what Jimmy had done.

"Did you ever hear him talk about his sister Amelia? I mean, besides that day?"

She shook her head. "No."

"How about Bud? Did he ever talk about her?"

She looked at me sharply. "He doesn't exactly talk about his past."

"Even after a few drinks?"

"When is he not drinking?"

I tilted my head. "Touché. Has he ever done anything to make you think he'd be capable of such an act?"

Her eyes turned narrow. Angry. She plunged into silence. I should have known she was too smart to step into any trap I'd lay for her. She still hadn't confessed that Bud was abusing her—and come to think of it, trying to trick her into saying something probably hadn't been the right move. The warning look was her only retribution.

Since dishonesty had failed, there was nothing left but the truth. "Bailey, I'm worried about you. I don't want you to end up like Amelia, okay? We're investigating Bud for some very serious crimes. I'm going to talk to social services and see if I can get you a new placement." When she was silent, I tried to find her eyes. "Do you understand what I'm saying?"

She nodded, emotionless.

"Are you okay with that?" I didn't really care if she was or wasn't. She wasn't staying with Bud anymore.

Her only response was a shrug. Ironically, it felt like progress. Previously, she had been against leaving Bud. My best guess was that she feared punishment. That was usually the reason people protected their abusers.

"Bailey. I'm not going to leave you."

That one seemed to take a moment to sink in, as if the concept were a little foreign.

"I'm seeing this thing through, and I'm not giving up until I see you in a beautiful, loving family, do you hear me? I'm going to be there on your adoption day, when the judge signs the paperwork. I'm going to be there the day you realize what love looks like and what it means to be precious to someone, okay?" I wasn't sure what led me to choose the word, but my voice caught as I said it. "I'm making you a promise."

A tear glittered in her eye, and I was afraid I'd said too much. But maybe tears were a good thing. Shedding a chrysalis that didn't fit anymore couldn't be pain-free.

And now I'd made a promise. A very thorough, specific one. To my shock, this one didn't scare me spitless, as they usually did. I somehow knew, in the pit of my stomach, that this was a promise I would finally keep.

I gave her several moments, and when she said nothing, I balled the empty chip bag. "You working the next tour?"

She nodded, her expression vacant.

"Good." Any time not spent with Bud Weber was good time. "I want you to stay safe, okay?"

Another nod.

"Okay." I bounced my heel, but there seemed to be nothing more to discuss. I stood up. "I'll be in touch."

She offered half a smile—a friendly gesture. A plea for me to go and leave her to her own thoughts.

So, I left, praying to God that something I'd said had finally broken through to her dark, hollow world.

CHAPTER TWENTY-THREE
TOMMY

———◉———

Propped up by frilly, embroidered pillows, I stared at the opposite wall, pale peach with sconces that held trailing vines. A Thomas Kinkade painting stared back at me, depicting a cottage that glowed beside a gently rippling river.

Lying around wasn't my idea of a good time. My mind was on the Mailboat. At every minute of the morning, I knew where it was. Mentally, I reminded Brian that the Wilsons asked for packages to be left inside their boat; the wind on that part of the lake blew them right off the pier. And he needed to be careful in the subdivision run where the water was only five feet deep. Did he remember to reverse the screws regularly to clear the lake weed from the propeller blades? The other boats rarely had to worry about that; they didn't spend as much time so close to shore. I shuddered to think of the repair list he was leaving for me, when the boats moved to the docks in Willams Bay for the winter. I pictured everything from scratched paint to a broken rudder to—

Cracked glass. The bullet had barely missed my head. Shards like ice rained down on the back of my neck. The gun spit again. Lead hit wood with a hollow thud, as if the wounded slab of pine had pulled in a sharp gasp. The boat took a third round with a brittle crack of plastic, the snap of tiny electric arcs.

The next slug hammered me below the rib.

I dropped.

No. No. The walls were pale peach. I could see them. Vaguely. I could smell the raspberry air freshener plugged into the outlet. Yes, but not as strongly as—

The smell of lemon floor cleaner. It filled my nostrils. The pain was hot. White hot. The boat was suddenly silent except for the sound of my own breathing. Ragged. Agonized.

A shadow leaned over me. "Want any more, Tommy?"

I grit my teeth against the pain. "Please..." My vision swam. The light was in my eyes. I couldn't make out his face. Only a black leather vest with silver studs.

He laughed. "You'll bleed out before she gets here."

My heart pounded. He knew Bailey was coming. "Don't hurt her," I gasped.

He chuckled again. "Don't worry, Tommy. I won't."

A shout left my lips. "Bailey!"

The sound of my own voice snapped me back into the pale peach room. It had three dimensions again. Substance. Weight. I could feel the bed sheets and the down pillows. My heart was pounding. Sweat drenched my shirt. My breath raced.

Thank God Nancy and Wade were at work. Their burying me under mountains of helpful concern was the last thing I needed. And I didn't care to explain why I had yelled. What had I even said? I wasn't sure. I had an uncomfortable feeling it was Bailey's name. Well. Even more reason to be glad I was alone.

The therapist at Froedtert Hospital looked up from my chart after peppering me with a dozen questions. "Tommy, you're at pretty high risk for PTSD. Have you had any nightmares? Flashbacks?"

I'd lied to him. No. None. Well, it wasn't like they were so bad. I figured they'd go away soon enough.

They hadn't.

I should call him.

But I was already exhausted by the three days a week I was taking PT. I just wanted this nightmare behind me so I could get on with life. Get back to the Mailboat. Get back to Bailey.

Was she okay? Why had I heard nothing from her since that day at the hospital? Was Bud Weber beating her up again? Wade assured me there were no new reports. Well, of course there weren't. *I* was the one reporting her bruises.

I eyed my phone, charging on the end table. There was barely room for it amidst the flurry of cards, bouquets, and stuffed animals from well-wishers. I'd avoided texting Bailey or even calling her. The things we had to talk about deserved to be said face-to-face, not over a phone. And besides, I had no idea why she was avoiding me, unless she objected that strongly to being a blood relative of mine.

I chewed my lip, then picked up my cell. I couldn't stand the silence and inaction any longer.

CHAPTER TWENTY-FOUR
BAILEY

———— ⛵ ————

I was glad I was working concessions for the next tour. So far, the passengers were happy in their little plastic chairs, every head turned toward the shoreline while they listened to Captain Brian's narration. They wouldn't want chips and soda until Williams Bay or even Fontana. So, I sat on my bench behind the counter on the aft deck, elbows on knees, and twirled my phone mid-air. In my brain, I replayed the things Ryan had said.

He wasn't going to leave me.

He was going to take me away from Bud.

He was going to be there someday when I got adopted.

He almost made it sound like he took the permanent position at the police department specifically so he could be around for me. But that was a ridiculous notion, straight out of that part of my brain that used to daydream that my dad was going to rescue me someday. My dad was just shipwrecked in the Antarctic or something, fighting his way through shifting sea ice and yawning crevasses. Looking forward to warmer weather and a hot meal and holding his little girl tight.

But I knew now that my dad was Jason Thomlin and that he'd been a bank burglar. And he hadn't even known I existed. Not until the night he was murdered in front of me. And when he was dying right there on the street beside me, he didn't even tell me who he was.

I got to spend one night with my dad. Just one night. When knowing my dad was all I ever wanted.

Was I supposed to be mad at him? And if so, for what? For not telling me? Or should I back up even further and be mad at him for not even knowing I was a thing? For making me by accident, then abandoning me to a life of misery and pointlessness? Was he even sorry?

And if I *should* be mad at him... Why wasn't I? Why was God the only person I was mad at, for not even letting me have five minutes with my dad and know that it was him?

And then I realized my phone was ringing. I quit spinning it and looked at the screen. It said CAPTAIN TOMMY. The profile pic was from a screenshot of a news article. He and I were standing next to each other on the rub board after tryouts this spring. We both looked so happy. So clueless about everything that would happen this summer. Why had I chosen such a dumb picture? That was back when I daydreamed he could be like a grandpa to me—never imagining he actually was.

I stared at the picture and the little ringing bell icon. Why was he calling me? We hadn't spoken since that day at the hospital. Did I want to talk to him now? Did I want to start thinking of him as my for-actual grandpa? Did I want to accept that Jason Thomlin was my dad and that I'd lost the chance to know him forever?

No.

That was a lot to ask of a girl.

I just wanted to think.

To find my feelings in this whole mess—if they even existed anymore.

127

I set my phone on the counter and stared at the picture of me and Tommy until the phone stopped ringing and the picture disappeared.

CHAPTER TWENTY-FIVE
TOMMY

The line rang half a dozen times before she picked up.

"Hey, this is Bailey."

Heart pounding, I opened my mouth to respond, but she spoke over me.

"Sorry I can't pick up right now, but if you leave me a message, I'll get back to you as soon as possible." There was a pause. "All right, 'bye." And then the tone sounded.

My first instinct was to hang up, my mind reverting to the notion that what we needed was a good, long talk—in person. But then I cast up how many weeks had gone by since we last spoke, and how many weeks were likely to go by before I could return to the Mailboat. Would I even make it back before the end of the summer? If not, was I willing to let all winter pass without speaking to her?

"Hey, Bailey," I said, my voice feeling scratchy and uncertain. "How ya doin'? Haven't heard from you in a while." I paused. Was I rambling? What was I supposed to say? "I hope you're okay. I think we've got some things to talk about. Call me…. Okay, I'll talk to you later."

I hung up. Laid my phone in my lap and stared at it. *Would* she call me later? Or would she go on ignoring me? I guess I'd forced the question at this point. If she never returned my call, then she was, in fact, ignoring me on purpose.

From the kitchen came the sound of the door opening and closing. Keys jangling. "Yoo-hoo! Tommy, you ready for PT?" It was Nancy.

Physical therapy. The current bane of my existence. I'd met my cheerful young therapist at the local clinic for the first time yesterday, and I wasn't sure how we were supposed to get along—not when she celebrated all my gains in mobility as if I were a toddler again. At my age, I didn't appreciate getting sent back to square one.

I glanced at the calendar on the opposite wall. July fifteenth. School started in a month and a half, and Bailey's hours would be drastically cut back. In eight weeks, marine mail delivery would end, and she'd be more likely to be scheduled on other boats besides mine, her specialized skill set no longer a determining factor. We'd have fewer chances to talk.

Setting my jaw, I threw back the covers and eased my legs out of the bed. The ache in my side was still there, despite the meds.

Nancy appeared in the doorway. Her name tag from Blackpoint Estate, the historic house where she was a tour guide, was still pinned to her blouse. Seeing me upright, she stopped and folded her arms. "Well, look at you!" She smiled with pleasure.

I waved to the hallway, where she had parked the walker the hospital had saddled me with. "Well, grab my contraption."

"Aye, aye, Captain." She turned to shuffle it into my room.

I wasn't going to lie here the whole rest of the summer. One way or another, I was making it back to the Mailboat. I was not letting Bailey drift away from me.

CHAPTER TWENTY-SIX
BAILEY

———— ✦ ————

My phone blinked at me, and a notification popped up, saying I had a new voicemail. Feeling a detached curiosity—just my grandpa calling, no big deal—I tapped the notification and typed in my PIN.

"Hey, Bailey." Tommy's warm voice filled the aft deck. It sort of counted as the first time he'd been on the Mailboat in weeks. He asked how I was doing. He told me to call him. He sounded like he missed me.

I snorted and put my phone to sleep. That was the kind of thing old me would have believed in: That someone cared about me. That I was special for once in my life.

But seriously, I'd been smacked awake too many times to fall for that crap anymore. Family were people who left you. If I were special, my dad would have told me who he was, and then he would have survived instead of dying in front of me. Or at the very least, he would have told me he loved me.

But no.

He died.

He left me.

Maybe I *was* a little mad at him.

Anyway, it was going to be a good, long time before I believed Tommy was really going to be there for me.

Maybe forever.

Until then, he could talk to my voicemail.

CHAPTER TWENTY-SEVEN
RYAN

———— ⚓ ————

Elkhorn. The county seat. I wended my way through hallways that felt familiar. I'd followed the same wall-mounted directories eleven years ago, the night I'd dropped off a tiny little girl with big, brown eyes.

It was easy to remember the showdown between the arguing couple, each of them high as a kite. It was impossible to forget the wide-eyed five-year-old I'd found hiding in a closet. I would always recall that she shed no tears, even as I carried her down this hallway on my hip.

Eleven years ago, I turned Bailey Johnson over to the system, not exactly hoping her mother would figure her life out; naively believing Bailey would be adopted quickly into a loving family.

How had it gone so wrong?

I quickly silenced the voice insisting her situation was my fault. I was getting better at turning down the burden of blame. Bill Gallagher had ruthlessly pointed out that my self-pity was helping no one. The only thing that would help was taking action.

Today, I was more than ready for action. I wasn't leaving until I had assurances Bailey would be placed in a new home. *Today.*

I imagined she might be shuffled anywhere in the county, depending where social services had an available foster home. And she didn't have a car, so that probably meant she'd have to quit her job at the Mailboat. By extension then, she'd see less of Tommy—and that was a problem to iron out. I wasn't sure what had fallen out between them, but I still believed in my gut that he was a key connection somehow.

One thing at a time. First, I just needed to get her away from Bud Weber.

I found the door I was looking for. It pulled me strongly back to that night. I stared at it. Told myself I was finally making restitution. That Bailey's torment ended today. I pushed it open.

"Can I help you, officer?"

A large, comfortable woman sat behind the desk, wearing a flouncy polka-dot dress. She smiled warmly behind horn-rimmed glasses. Something about her reminded me of my favorite teacher from grade school. The nameplate on the edge of her desk said *Betty Evans.*

"Yes, I need to speak with the case worker for one of your fosters, Bailey Johnson."

"Certainly. One moment." She clacked on her keyboard with bright red manicured nails, her fingers blinged out with oversized rings. After a moment of searching, her face fell. "Oh." She chewed her lip, looking uncomfortable, as if she'd opened the door to the craft closet, only to find every piece of paper stuck to the wall with glue sticks. "I'm afraid Bailey's case worker isn't available. Would you like to speak with our director?"

"All the better."

The woman rose with a relieved smile. "I'll see if she's available. May I ask the purpose of your visit today?"

"Bailey's foster dad is currently under investigation for some very serious allegations. I'm here to see about getting Bailey rehomed."

The smile withered, but the woman concealed it with a quick nod. "Wait here, please."

She vanished down a hall, leaving me to stand, hands on my duty belt, staring at literature about how to become a foster parent. A man, a woman, and a child, bathed in sunlight, laughed joyously from the front of the brochure. I couldn't help thinking the advertising was off.

And for some reason, I couldn't help grabbing a copy and tucking it into my pocket.

I went on to study the furniture, the carpet, the adorable ceramic pig on the receptionist's desk—all while wondering if she was ever coming back. Was it me, or was she taking a long time?

At last, she reappeared, smiling warmly again—maybe because I was happily no longer her problem.

"The director will see you now."

I fell into step behind the woman, who led me down the hall. The receptionist stopped at a door and knocked brightly, then pushed it open and waved me in.

A tall woman stood from behind her desk, her brown hair piled artfully in carefree waves, her efficient form clad in a blazer and pencil skirt. She reached across the desk to shake my hand. "Good afternoon, Officer. I'm Michelle Stafford." Her handshake was firm and her manner of speech efficient.

"Thanks for seeing me. I'm Officer Brandt."

"Have a seat." She waved me to a chair, then sat and folded her hands on her desk. "I understand you have some concerns about one of our foster homes."

I settled into the seat offered to me. "Yes. Bud Weber."

"Would you please elaborate?"

"His foster ward, Bailey Johnson, has had some bruises no one can explain."

135

Ms. Stafford turned to her computer and clicked her mouse. "How old is the child?"

"Sixteen."

"Have you asked her how she came by her bruises?"

I shrugged. "She says she ran into stuff."

She looked at me over her glasses, her gaze pointed. "You don't believe her?"

I stopped, jaw slack. Surely she knew that "running into stuff" was the go-to explanation from every victim of domestic violence ever. In a heartbeat, what I'd taken to be a professional conversation had turned antagonistic—and I was the bad guy, or at least the bumbling cop.

She reached into a drawer and pulled out a sheet of paper, then laid it on the desk in front of me. "If you'd like to file a formal complaint, we'll look into it."

I wondered what "looking into it" entailed. I'd already interviewed Bud and Bailey—multiple times—and run a background check on Bud and was currently making him the focus of a full-scale investigation.

And I *still* had no concrete evidence. In light of that, what would this woman who didn't believe me accomplish?

I took the sheet, meeting Ms. Stafford's eye. "I *will* file a complaint. But the things I'm here to talk about go way past paperwork. Weber is currently under investigation for very serious allegations. We consider Bailey's safety at risk. I'm here to request she be removed to a new foster home— today."

"I'm afraid that would be very difficult."

"Difficult? We suspect Bud Weber of the rape and murder of a female minor."

She adjusted her glasses, her motion precise and practiced. "Has Mr. Weber been convicted of a felony?"

"No. The investigation is ongoing."

"Then I'm afraid we don't have sufficient grounds to revoke his foster care license."

"Are you kidding me?"

136

"No. We take the rights of our foster care providers very seriously."

"And in the process, you sacrifice the child. How is that right?"

"I'm not paid to decide what's right, Officer Brandt. I'm paid to provide child protective services within the legal framework as it stands."

"Ms. Stafford, I am an officer of the law. You won't even take *my* word that this home is unsafe?"

"It's not a matter of whether or not I believe you. It's a matter of what can be proved."

I leaned forward and tapped my fingers on the desk. "Technically, it's your job to determine whether a foster home is safe."

She smiled coldly and nodded at the document she'd handed me. "If you file the complaint, I promise I'll look into it."

"Fine. Yes. I'm submitting the paperwork. But I'm also going to continue my investigation on Weber. And I recommend you let me know what kind of coffee you like, because I'm going to be in this room *every day* presenting my findings until you have no choice but to care."

Her eyes turned to ice, her professional demeanor vanishing, the real woman suddenly and violently showing through. *"Don't* suggest I don't care."

Her outburst left me speechless—not only because of her passion but because I still couldn't reconcile her statement with the evidence to the contrary.

She composed herself, smoothing down her skirt, then added, "As someone who works at the intersection of the law and human nature, I should think you'd understand. I receive complaints every single day—from biological parents and family members, from adoptive parents, from the children themselves. Most are unfounded. The minute you take a child from their birth family, absolutely no one is happy about it and absolutely no one is civil. The worst kind of accusations ensue from all parties involved. I spend all day trying to sort these out."

Her position began to run clear. "I'm assuming it would be impractical to move a child temporarily until the investigation was resolved."

"Yes. For two reasons. One, every time you rehome a child, you only add to their trauma. Two, where am I going to put her? To be frank, there is nowhere for Bailey to go."

"You don't have a home waiting for a child? Maybe even some nice couple looking to adopt?" Somehow in my mind, I had pictured dozens of families eager to fall in love with a new kid, especially one as sweet as Bailey.

The director folded her hands patiently. "Officer Brandt, on an average day in Wisconsin, the number of kids in need of a home outnumber foster homes four to one. We are maxed out. As for adoptive parents—not to be a pessimist, but Bailey's too old. People want babies and toddlers—kids too young to be 'tainted' by the system. Teens in foster care have usually been here half their lives. They're scarred, and they're working through a lot of trauma. And so, there are rumors. As far as adopters are concerned, Bailey Johnson is more likely to murder them in their sleep than become a natural fit for their family."

My jaw went slack. "Bailey's the victim in all this. She's just a kid—a *really good* kid." I tried to forget that one time she looked like she was ready to deck me.

"I'm merely explaining the facts to you as they stand."

I slumped in my chair and released a heavy sigh. I'd had no idea just how steeply the odds were stacked against Bailey's favor. No wonder she was still trapped in the system. No wonder she was stuck with Bud Weber. The entire foster care system, in its current desperate state, was a more perfect environment for child predators than for children.

I sighed and rubbed my forehead, trying to wrangle my thoughts. "Okay. All right. I'll, uh… I'll file the complaint,

138

and I'll continue my investigation." I met her eyes, changing my tone. "And I'll share with you whatever I find."

"I can't revoke a license without good cause," she said firmly.

"I understand. I'll do my best." Meekly, I rose and made for the door.

"Officer."

Hand on the knob, I turned.

She twisted a pen in her hands, elbows on her desk, her eyes studying me as if she were trying to make up her mind. At last, she sighed and flipped up a palm. "I take tea, not coffee."

I smiled. That was as much as an invitation as I was going to get, and you better believe I was going to take it. In fact, I was going to try every variety of the best-brewed tea in the county until I figured out which one she liked best.

I left her office, wandered back to the lobby, and scowled at the document I was to fill out. Paperwork. This wasn't what I'd come here for. Bailey deserved more.

I sat down and poured my soul into that document, stacking every fact I knew and most of what I suspected— everything I could without compromising the investigation. When I was done, I sighed, rose, and approached the receptionist, Betty.

Her smile was genuine but demure, as if she knew what kind of conversation had happened behind the closed door. "Thank you, officer. I'll pass this back to Ms. Stafford right away."

"I appreciate that." I turned to leave.

"Um…"

I paused. Betty was biting the end of a pencil, staring at her desk as if trying to make up her mind. She lifted her eyes, looked at me, then pulled a sheet of paper from the corner of her desk.

"I'm not sure I should do this, but… I made you a list of Bailey's past case workers."

I took it eagerly. There were at least a dozen names. "So many?"

"It's hard to keep them. The work is very… Well, it's stressful. Most places have a fairly high turnover rate."

I nodded. It fit the picture that was coming together for me. The train wreck that I was just discovering was the environment these people worked in every day. And this list of names was one more reason why Bailey continued to flounder in foster care. No one knew her story from beginning to end except what they each read in impersonal documentation. It wasn't the same as walking her journey alongside her, knowing what she needed intuitively.

"Who's her current case worker?" I asked.

Betty chewed her lip, as she had the first time I asked. "Anna Clapton was the most recent. She left us about a month ago."

"So who's her worker now?"

"Technically she's with Chloe White, just until we fill Anna's position. But Chloe hasn't had a chance to meet with Bailey yet, so…" She trailed off.

So Bailey didn't even have a proper case worker right now. And she hadn't since I'd crossed paths with her this summer. I decided not to comment. Offloading my frustrations on the receptionist wasn't going to solve the problems she already seemed well aware of.

I carefully folded the list of names she'd given me. "Thank you. I appreciate this."

She nodded meekly. She didn't seem to have the heart to apply more words to the situation.

I left. I was sure I was going to see a lot more of that office. I was sure I was going to feel this same sick, twisted feeling in my gut every time I was there.

I just hoped I could save Bailey in time before anything happened to her. I'd made a promise to her today—a promise to be there when she was adopted into a real family.

But now I understood what she'd known all along: I had promised her something utterly impossible.

WEDNESDAY
JULY 16, 2014

CHAPTER TWENTY-EIGHT
ANGELICA

—————✦—————

Angelica's heart pounded with every step from her hotel to the Lake Geneva Police Station. Was this the right move? What if she ran into Wade Erickson himself? Did he know who she was? What if he demanded to know what she was doing at the police station? What she was doing in Lake Geneva?

But where else could she find information on what had happened the night Bobby Markham was killed? Every original record was housed in this very building. There was no way around this.

Trembling, she pulled open the front door and stepped into the atrium. To her left was a glassed-in window like the one at the county courthouse. But this one had a phone mounted to the wall with a sign instructing her to pick it up for service.

She peered through the glass. Rows of desks were piled with computer monitors. Only one was currently manned, the one at the very back. The woman wore a headset and typed at a furious pace while staring at her screens and speaking into her microphone.

Slightly afraid of interrupting, Angelica lifted the phone from its cradle and pressed it to her ear. It rang. The woman on the opposite side of the room pressed a button and her voice came through the line. Her eyes met Angelica's across the room and through the glass. "How can I help you?"

"I would like to make an open records request?" Angelica said, her voice scratchy.

"Of course. I'll be with you in a moment."

Angelica nodded and hung up the phone. She folded her hands on the counter, one on top of the other. But her heart pounded in her chest. She just wanted to fill out whatever request form they handed her and be done with it.

The main door opened behind her, and a man stepped through. Seeing her waiting at the counter, he simply took his place behind her in line. Angelica would have preferred he weren't there, even though she told herself it shouldn't matter. Still, she felt as if the fewer people who saw her here, the better.

She studied his reflection in the glass. Tall, narrow, his dark brown hair highlighted blond. He wore pressed slacks with a belt and a plaid, button-down shirt. His style was sharp, and Angelica approved. With one hand in his pocket, he waited his turn, scrolling his phone. His lack of attention on her helped calm her nerves. It would be fine. It didn't matter he was there.

The dispatcher finally rose from her desk, approached the glass, and pulled a sheet of paper from an organizer mounted to the wall. Angelica's heart rate went right back up. This was a small department. Would Wade Erickson hear that someone was asking questions about Bobby Markham's death?

The woman laid the paper down, ready to point sections out and explain. But to Angelica, the general layout of the document already looked familiar. So did the sense of fear that, like last time, she would somehow be thwarted,

145

nothing coming of her efforts. After all, would Wade Erickson still be walking free if the documents related to his case were this easy to access?

She held up a hand to stop the woman. "I'm looking for information on the Markham Ring—specifically on Bobby Markham's shooting." She was careful not to mention Erickson by name. "*Are* those records open to the public?"

The woman narrowed her eyes. Was it just Angelica, or did she detect a hint of caution? Did the dispatcher know more than she was willing to say? In all likelihood, this small department was abuzz with the words "Markham Ring," thanks to the murders so recently associated with it. Had Angelica tipped her hand? Ruined her chance?

"I'm with the press," she blurted. She wasn't even sure how or why she thought of it.

The woman seemed to accept her statement—to Angelica's relief. Of course, if the dispatcher had asked, she would have been incapable of providing credentials proving she worked for any media outlet.

"I wouldn't know whether those records specifically are open to the public," the woman replied. "But if you fill out the form, we can check. Your publication won't be charged for anything but our time."

Angelica glanced at the sheet. Like the one at the county courthouse, it asked for her name, address, and phone number. It would likely take the staff several days to dig up the records. Angelica would need to have them mailed to her address in Malibu—either her home or her office. Would the dispatcher believe that a publication all the way on the west coast had taken an interest in this story? Worse, did Angelica dare leave her calling card—and instructions on where to find her—under Wade Erickson's very nose?

Movement within the dispatch center caught her eye, shifting her focus. Two men walked into the room bearing Styrofoam cups. They leaned against a set of cabinets and began to chat, as if the dispatch center were their unofficial break room. One of the men wore a black polo shirt and tan pants and had spiky gray hair. She recognized him as the man who had gotten into a car with Monica Steele the other day—her partner, perhaps?

The other was half a head taller and wore a navy-blue uniform with gold trim. His facial features were firmly chiseled. His eyes intense, even as he shot the breeze with his co-worker. Angelica's heart stopped.

Wade Erickson.

He had barely seemed to age from the photos she'd seen in the newspaper. His hair had grayed, his build was perhaps a shade heavier—that was all. There was no mistaking it was him.

He lifted his cup to his mouth. Raised his eyes toward the glass. Their gazes met. Like a deer caught in the headlights, Angelica couldn't look away. Erickson merely looked at her with detached curiosity. Maybe he didn't know who she was, and he was wondering why she was staring. Maybe he knew *exactly* who she was but could put on a brilliant act for the benefit of Steele's partner.

"Ma'am?" The dispatcher broke into her thoughts. "Would you still like to fill out the form?"

Angelica tore her eyes away from Erickson and stared at the sheet, the empty boxes swimming before her eyes. Did Erickson know who she was? What she looked like? Had he researched every detail of Will's life—including his wife? His children? At the thought of her husband's murderer knowing the faces of her boys, ice cracked its way up her spine, sending her mind into a panic. She felt long, thin hands closing around her throat...

"No," she told the dispatcher. "No. Never mind. Thank you."

She backed away from the window, almost stepping on the feet of the man behind her. She muttered a quick apology and pushed through the door. The outside air and

147

the sunlight greeted her as if she had been suffocating. She rushed down the sidewalk, stealing backward glances, paranoid someone might be following her—but she saw no one besides an elderly couple strolling arm-in-arm.

Stupid, stupid, stupid! What had she been thinking, walking in there? Had Erickson recognized her? Would the dispatcher tell him what Angelica had asked for? Would he understand she suspected him? What would be the repercussions? Had she just painted a blazing target on her back? On the backs of her sons?

She broke into a run and didn't stop until she reached her hotel room. Once she was there, she double bolted the door, collapsed against it, and buried her face in her hands.

She needed to talk to Roland.

She pulled her phone out of her purse. Dialed his number. It rang. And rang. Finally, the line clicked.

"Hello," a refined voice said.

"Roland—"

He spoke over the top of her. "—you have reached the voicemail of Roland Markham. Please leave a message and I'll get back to you as soon as possible."

A tone beeped.

Angelica hung up and let her phone drop to her side, her head leaning against the door. She stared at the ceiling, her heart still pounding. What was she going to do?

CHAPTER TWENTY-NINE
SKULL

Humored by Angelica Read nearly running him over on her way out of the police station, Skull took note of which direction she ran. Her hotel. He'd follow her in a moment. For now, he pocketed his phone and approached the service window.

"How can I help you?" the dispatcher asked.

Skull offered a warm, professional smile. "Hello, I'm new in town. I'll be teaching fourth grade at Central-Denison, and I was wondering about having one of your officers speak to my class this fall?"

The dispatcher smiled. "Oh, of course." She grabbed a flier and paused to write something on the cover. "You should talk to Sergeant Brown. He'll be happy to set you up. I'm writing his hours. Just call the front desk, and we'll put you through to him when he's on duty." She slid it through the glass.

Skull took it and used it to offer a friendly wave. "Thank you. I can't wait."

He walked out the door. His whole time in the lobby, he'd been careful to never make eye contact with Wade Erickson. The Man wouldn't approve.

He wouldn't have needed to follow Angelica inside in the first place, except that keeping a bug on her was practically impossible. He'd dropped one into her purse the first day of the tail—but it turned out Angelica Read changed handbags as often as her makeup. A fashionista was a damn hard target to follow.

Once outside, Skull scanned the street and noted that Angelica hadn't gotten far. She was just rounding the corner a few blocks away, straight for her hotel, as he had guessed. He followed at a more leisurely pace. He didn't need to be seen again. Still, the risk had paid off. Her stress over wanting case records so badly—then abandoning them altogether—was very telling. He could smell her fear. The Man could use fear.

Of course, Skull hadn't known Erickson would be there. The Man might berate him later. He hoped not. This was a good gig. He didn't want to lose it.

Or become The Man's next target.

He gave The Man good information. Details. Nuances. After The Man's interest had been piqued by the boy Jimmy Beacon, it was Skull who had brought to his attention the fact that Beacon and Bud Weber were unwittingly connected by the murder of Beacon's sister. Skull was a finder and knower of facts. And he could connect facts, putting them into the right hands at the right time—for the right price.

He had, of course, told The Man about the electric enmity between Delilah Beacon and Monica Steele. But The Man had merely appeared to file the information, plugging it into whatever puzzle, whatever grand plan, he was building in his mind.

And then he had instructed Skull to continue following Angelica Read.

So follow her he did. And now that he understood how obsessed she was with Wade Erickson—he knew why.

The Man was going to go to town.

CHAPTER THIRTY
ANGELICA

———————— ⚙ ————————

Roland's tone was apologetic over the phone. "My dear, I'm so sorry. The president of the board called an emergency meeting—the CEO retired. Health complications. I had to run to the city. It was all very last minute."

Angelica nodded, the lake breeze playing with her hair as she sat on a bench overlooking the marina. "I understand. Don't think of it."

"I should be back tomorrow. I'll take you to lunch. We'll discuss everything then. In detail."

She smiled. "Thank you." There was so much she wanted to go over with Roland.

She heard a voice in the background on his end. Then Roland spoke through the line again. "I'm so sorry, my dear. I have to get back to the board room. I'll see you at lunch tomorrow."

"See you then."

They hung up. Angelica sighed and gazed across the lake. Her investigation already felt as if it were at a dead end. She hoped Roland could help her find the trail. In the meanwhile, she had a full day to herself—and no idea what she was going to do with it.

She should call her mamá. Talk to her boys. See how they were doing. Lifting her phone, she speed-dialed her mother.

The line picked up. The voice of her nine-year-old son Mason came through. "Hi, Mom!"

Joy filled her chest. "Hello, Mason! How are you?"

"Good. I miss you, Mom. Are you coming home soon?"

Sadness tweaked her heartstrings. She'd been gone almost a week. "Soon, honey. You and Abuela are picking me up from the airport this weekend, remember?"

He sighed dramatically. "That's a really long time."

"Aren't you having fun with Abuela and Abuelo?"

"Yeeeaaah." He dragged the word out like a tire losing air.

"What's the matter, honey?"

He sighed again. His voice was tiny when he replied. "Kyle said my dad was a bad man, and it was okay he died."

Fury built in Angelica's chest. "Kyle Watson?"

"Yeah."

Angelica ground her teeth and bounced her crossed legs. This wasn't the first time the Watsons, her parents' neighbors, had dropped unfeeling remarks in front of her children, and the parents were just as guilty as the kids. "Well, you know what? You don't have to play with Kyle anymore. Okay?"

"Okay," Mason mumbled.

Her mamá's voice called from the background in Spanish. *Mijo,* is that your mamá?"

Mason hesitated before muttering, *"Sí..."*

"Did you tell her what happened?"

He hesitated even longer. "Sí..."

"Did you tell her *everything?*"

"...No..."

Angelica frowned. "Mason, what happened?"

The silence lingered so long, Angelica knew her son was in trouble, and merely trying to stave off the inevitable.

152

"I kneed Kyle in the balls."

Angelica's jaw dropped. "You *what?*" She'd never imagined her son doing such a thing.

The phone clattered as if changing hands. "Go outside. Go." Abuela spoke to Angelica next. *"Mija.* Where are you? When are you coming home?"

Somehow, Angelica felt as if she were the one in the hot seat now. "I'm coming home this weekend. Like we discussed."

"Make it tomorrow."

"Mamá?" After raising Angelica's two brothers, she couldn't imagine there was anything her mother couldn't handle.

"Angelica. Your sons need you. Kaydon? He sits and stares out the window. Mason? He gets into fights. They lost their papá. They don't need to lose their mamá, too."

Her words hit home deeply, tearing open her already-devastated heart. The last thing she needed was her mother telling her what a horrible parent she was.

"I'm trying to find out what *happened* to their papá."

"Phbttt, he was murdered. Leave it to the police."

Tears stung Angelica's eyes. Her mamá hadn't hated Will, but mostly she had loved his money. Now that he was dead and a wanted criminal, she had no love for him at all.

"Mamá, how can you say that?"

"With my mouth," she said bluntly. "If you prefer, I'll send it in a letter. Now. Are you coming home, or do I have to put the boys on an airplane for Chicago?"

Angelica closed her eyes. Her mamá would do it, too. She never made a threat she wasn't willing to follow through on.

"All right, all right. I'll check the flights. I'll come home as soon as possible."

"Gracias."

Her mamá sounded both gratified and grateful. She never minced her words, nor did she spare anyone's

153

feelings when she felt the truth needed a good airing. "Love you, *mijita.*"

"Love you, too, Mamá." And she meant it—hard as it was to admit sometimes.

She hung up and tilted her face to the sky. Her mother was right. Kaydon and Mason needed her. But she felt torn. She would not be able to live her life without knowing why her Will had died.

Metal clanged gently. Angelica noticed a nautical flagpole. The US flag was on top, pennants running down the sides in the shape of a triangle. She kept staring as the breeze played with the colorful fabrics, not sure why she was so fascinated. The image was quintessential of Lake Geneva.

The breeze wisped a leaf across the path in front of her, drawing her eye. The paved trail seemed to run infinitely in either direction along the shore. Her feet felt compelled to move. To follow.

She got up and walked, choosing the right-hand side at random. The path led past the marina, then plunged into the trees. From there, it seemed to open straight into someone's yard, switching from pavement to gravel. She wondered if it was okay to keep going, then noticed other walkers on the trail. Despite being so cozy with the lakeside houses—coming between them and their own piers—it was apparently a public walkway. Fascinated, she kept going.

The houses were immaculate, well-appointed on open green lawns. Shingle, Cape Cod, farmhouse—they were each beautifully executed. Some were clearly original to the late nineteenth and early twentieth centuries, flawlessly maintained or restored. Whether the main color was delft or beige or dove, white trim was a going theme, tying in with the white piers on the shore, adding to the air of light and leisure that embraced Lake Geneva.

The breeze caught Angelica's hair. Like a gentle hand, it caressed her face, pulling her attention toward the water. A bright yellow catamaran eased past, its sails full of the wind. She smiled. Roland had spoken of the catamaran that had been Bobby, Fritz, and Jason's pride and joy.

And then she noticed the young sailors out on the boat. Three pre-teen boys. She stared, feeling as if she were seeing a ghost from the past. The boys laughed and teased, but handled their craft expertly, tacking into the wind. She watched until they were a dot on the horizon.

The wind touched her face again, and with it, she thought she heard a voice.

Angelica.

The voice was Will's. It sounded not only like her husband, but like something that had sprung from the very ground she stood on, as if his voice and this lake vibrated to the same frequency. As if their souls were one and the same. As if this were the place he had always belonged.

I wanted so badly to bring you here.

She blinked and a tear rolled down her cheek. If Will had wanted to show her this place, why didn't he *say* something? Why did he lie to her? About everything? She whispered through gritted teeth. "You do not betray your family. You betrayed your own sons. You betrayed *me.*"

Some deep part of her mind continued to breathe the things she imagined Will would try to say to her.

I'm sorry. I never thought I'd have a family. Not after what I'd done. I tried so hard not to fall in love with you. I tried so hard...

It was true. The heat had been so strong, from the moment they met. And yet he'd taken an eternity to ask her out, after weeks of clumsily trying to avoid her.

Would it have been better if we'd never met? his voice seemed to ask, hesitating.

She thought of the moments they'd shared together, from the giddy highs of falling in love, to the lows of family

155

emergencies, to the mundane tasks of doing dishes together. She thought of her two boys. How Will had treated her like both a queen and an invalid for the entirety of each pregnancy. How he had been there for each delivery. How his eyes had glowed when he held his sons. How he had cried with her and kissed her with passion and joy.

And then she thought how every moment of that journey had been a complete and utter lie.

She locked her jaw as the tears came hot and fast, blurring her view of the lake.

"Yes," she spat out. "It would have been better if we never met."

CHAPTER THIRTY-ONE
BAILEY

———✦———

Who would have thought there was a website called "Find a Grave dot com"? But there is, and that's how I figured out where my dad was buried.

Though what had possessed me to look it up, I don't even know. It wasn't like I was ever going there.

On Wednesday morning, my day off, I pushed my bike out of the weeds growing beside Bud's garage, strapped on my helmet, and started pedaling. The cemetery was five miles outside of town. I'd never biked beyond the city limits before. But in a matter of minutes, I found myself pedaling along the shoulder of the highway like some health enthusiast, jumping out of my skin every time a car zipped by.

This was dumb. I told myself I could turn back whenever I felt like it. But I never did. I kept going. I told myself it was because the farms were pretty, with their silos and big, red barns.

Before I knew it, I was staring at an iron fence along the highway and the headstones beyond. I got off my bike and walked until I found the gate. Then I leaned my bike against a tree and started looking for fresh graves.

The first one wasn't it, but I got all nervous-excited anyway, just to find a totally different name on the temporary plaque. I didn't let myself get so worked up the next time, even though the name on a nearby stone said MARTA THOMLIN.

My stomach twisted into knots. Nearby stones said HENRY THOMLIN. ELAINA THOMLIN. SEBASTIAN THOMLIN.

I made a double take on the last one, my mind scrambling. Sebastian was Tommy's real name. It took me forever to notice there wasn't any end date. It was a double headstone, like for a husband and wife. The name on the left... Elaina. She'd died ten years ago.

I sat in the grass in front of the graves and wrapped my arms around my knees. So. This was my family. This was where I came from. Elaina, my grandmother. Henry. Maybe a great-uncle or something. Based on the dates, he was two years younger than Tommy and died young. And Marta? My great-grandmother. That tombstone was really old.

Did I seriously belong to these people?

And why did they all have to be dead?

I finally pulled together my courage and turned to the new grave. The one on the right. The dirt was heaped on top of it with sod rolled over that. A little brass plate read JASON THOMLIN.

Jason.

My dad.

For the next eternity and a half, I just sat there and stared. This was the guy I'd been looking for all my life. My hero who was supposed to swoop down and rescue me. He was supposed to explain that communist spies had been holding him captive for the past sixteen years, and that was the only reason he never came for me. But he'd escaped—past concrete walls and razor wire and search dogs and flood lights—and he'd combed the world over until he found me. And then he was supposed to bring me to a cozy

158

little cottage on the seashore with ivy growing up the chimney, and he was supposed to sit me down and hold me close and promise that he would never, never leave me again.

But he was dead.

Maybe replaying my fantasies was a bad idea. My eyes got all watery, and my nose started to run.

The newspapers said he was a bank burglar. A high-profile thief. A fugitive. A murderer. Even Tommy said so.

I didn't care what he was. I just wanted to know one thing.

I rubbed my nose on the back of my arm and tried to see anything past the curtains of tears now streaming from my eyes. My ears felt hot. My voice was in a noose. I croaked the words out anyway.

"Did you love me, Daddy?" That's all I'd ever wanted to know.

But of course, he'd never had the chance to love me or not.

THURSDAY
JULY 17, 2014

CHAPTER THIRTY-TWO
ANGELICA

Raindrops plinked the window beside Angelica's booth. She clutched a warm mug of coffee between her hands, studying the emblem of a red rooster and the words Egg Harbor Cafe. Every time the door opened, she looked up. But it was never Roland. She tapped the mug impatiently. He'd agreed to change their appointment to a morning meal, but he'd only gotten back to Lake Geneva late last night. She felt guilty rolling him out of bed.

Glancing through the rain-streaked window, she saw her rental car, waiting in a nearby stall. She'd return it to O'Hare later this morning. And then she'd board her plane for LAX. She was leaving Lake Geneva in a matter of hours. Worried as she was about Kaydon and Mason, her heart twinged a little at the thought of leaving this place, and not just because of her unfinished investigation.

Thanks largely to Roland, she'd gotten to know Lake Geneva in a different light than she'd expected—the way Will had known it. Not as the place where he had died, but the place where he had lived. Where he had grown up. Where he had laughed and played and made friends and built an entire life and dreamed of a future.

Forgiveness was still a long way off. But at least she had solved one mystery: the identity of the man she had married. She had context now. A depth of personal and family history she'd never known, in all their years together. It was something.

The bell above the cafe door rang. Angelica's eyes flashed upward. The patron who entered was Roland. She smiled and sighed in relief. She would get to speak with him one last time before she left.

He paused to talk with the hostess, who pointed out Angelica's table. He nodded, then hurried over. In honor of the weather, he'd donned a thicker sweater, cream-colored with knitted cables and carved wooden buttons. He slid into the booth opposite Angelica and reached for both her hands.

"My dear, I'm so glad I caught you before you left."

She smiled weakly. "I need to get home to my boys."

"Of course you must. Are you all right? You sounded distressed when we spoke over the phone."

She took a deep breath, then told him in more detail of her failed quests at the county courthouse and the police station. She described her terror at practically coming face-to-face with Wade himself. But nothing had happened since, so surely she was overthinking the encounter. Regardless, her investigation had reached a dead end, unless the county clerk in Elkhorn actually managed to find some documents that weren't tied up by secrecy laws. Even then, she'd have to be lucky enough for such a record to provide proof that Wade was, in fact, guilty of murder. Or that there had been a mistrial. Or a flaw in the investigation. And what were the odds of finding anything so obvious?

Deflated, Angelica leaned on her hand and stared across the table at her friend. "What do I do, Roland? I don't know where to go next."

He drummed his fingers together, a pensive look on his face. Then he cocked a smile. "For starters, we order breakfast. An investigation such as this really does call for a full stomach."

Angelica allowed an exhausted smile to slip across her face. He was probably right.

Roland ordered hash browns and fried eggs, sunny-side-up, while Angelica asked for toast and fruit. Once the waiter took the menus away, Roland folded his hands and looked Angelica squarely in the eye.

"First of all, I wouldn't discount a clue that isn't yet firmly in your hand. You don't know what your friend at the courthouse may turn up. Whatever she finds, it probably won't be a smoking gun in the hands of Wade Erickson." He tilted his head. "But it might point toward another door. A door you haven't tried yet. Don't give up too quickly."

Angelica nodded. Of course he was right. She wasn't known for her patience. She wanted the first door she opened to have all the answers.

"Second, we may not have to give up on those reports from the police station."

Angelica sat upright. "What do you mean? Is there still a chance?" She shrank into her seat again. "Roland, I don't think I can go back there."

He waved a finger. "Neither you nor I shall go anywhere near it. You forget, I have connections. Your media ruse wasn't a bad idea, but what if an actual reporter requested the records?"

Angelica's eyes widened. "Do you know someone?"

Roland grinned and twiddled his thumbs. "I believe I have an old favor I can call in. The man could get secrets from a marble statue. If those documents can be had, they will be had. Frankly, I don't know why we didn't try this in the first place."

Tears nearly threatened to fall. "Roland, you're wonderful."

He waved a hand. "Don't thank me yet. There's still every chance that, despite all our efforts, we may come up empty-handed. Should that prove the case…" He spread his palms. "Where shall we turn next? We may as well plan our moves ahead of time."

Angelica rested her chin on her hands, fingers laced, and searched the corners of the room for ideas. "The shootout, the end of the Markham Ring—this was a major case. Would other agencies have helped with the investigation?" Police departments did that sort of thing, didn't they? Crime reports in the papers always ended with a list of agencies that were assisting.

"In fact, I believe other agencies *were* involved," said Roland. "The Walworth County Sheriff's Office, as a matter of course. Chicago, Milwaukee, Madison—their departments would have wanted their fingers in the pie; it was their banks that were broken into. Perhaps a smattering of other agencies, both local and state. I'll have my reporter friend inquire after them all."

"You're wonderful." Another idea leapt to Angelica's mind. "We should speak with Jason's father, Tommy."

Roland leaned back, an expression of warning on his face. "That may not get you where you think it will."

She frowned. "Why not?"

"Wade and I may have parted ways, but he and Tommy have always remained close."

"How close?"

"I have it from the grapevine that Tommy is spending his recovery at Wade's house."

Angelica stared at Roland, slack-jawed. "But Wade was the one who shot him!"

Roland twisted his head and spoke haltingly, as if the full horror of the situation were forming in his mind. "If Wade is the missing fourth member, then yes."

Angelica reached for his wrist. "You have to talk to him. To warn him. He has to get out of that house."

Roland leaned back, pressing his fingers to his chest. "But will he believe me? They've been best friends since they were boys. They're more than brothers to each other. And once again, we lack evidence. How am I to convince him?"

Angelica shrugged. "Maybe you don't need to. Ask him to find out for himself." She leaned forward and pressed her finger into the table. "He's in Wade's house. Maybe there's evidence. Ask him to look."

"Recruit him?" Roland's expression was dubious. "I'll do my best, but I make no promises."

Angelica shook her head. "You have to try. Tommy's in danger as long as he's in that house."

Roland nodded somberly.

Angelica leaned back in her booth, satisfied that she'd won that argument. "Who else can we talk to?"

Roland twirled his thumbs. "Monica Steele may prove an invaluable ally."

Angelica stiffened. "The detective?"

"That's right. Do you know her?"

"She flew out to California to interview me after Will's death."

"Did she?"

Angelica nodded, memories of the woman's coolness spinning icicles in her brain. "I don't like her."

"Whyever not?"

"She's a cold, heartless bitch—pardon my French."

Roland's mouth initially fell open, and then he quirked his head, conceding her point. "Well, I can't say you're wrong..."

Angelica nodded conclusively. "How do you know her?"

"Well, after your husband's remains were left on my property and a warning written in blood on my window, she's had occasion to come around."

Angelica nodded her head side-to-side. Fair. But the real question... "Do you trust her?"

166

"She is the most sensible, clear-sighted woman I know. She harbors no fools." He raised a finger. "Which is a vital point. She's Wade's protégé. Getting her to turn against him may prove no easier than Tommy."

Angelica raised her eyebrows in surprise, then shrugged, trying not to look too delighted. "Then we leave her out of it."

"Sooner or later, we may have no choice. Once we have evidence, who do we give it to?"

"Anyone. Another agency. The state police."

"And then what will happen to the evidence you paid your blood, sweat, and tears for? Will it be taken seriously—the findings of an untrained civilian? Will law enforcement prove reluctant to turn against its own? What if your evidence isn't conclusive? What if it's merely suggestive? What if it gets trapped in differences of opinion? Departmental politics? Bureaucratic nonsense? No. When you pass this baton, it needs to come to the hands of someone who will carry it over the finish line."

Angelica scowled. "And why is that Monica Steele? You said yourself, she's Wade's protégé."

Roland grinned. "You yourself described her as a 'cold, heartless bitch.' And that is what makes her the right woman for the job. She will never put a personal friendship, however close, above doing the right thing—of that, I'm sure. That woman has a moral code engraved in iron."

Angelica let the thought soak in. If Roland was right, then no doubt that was why Steele had been so heartless during their interview. Finding the truth was simply more important to her than catering to Angelica's raw emotions at the time. Still...

"I don't like her."

Roland dropped his chin and twirled his thumbs. "Fair. But when the time comes, I do hope you'll heed my advice."

"And until then, I hope you won't let her know we had this conversation—or any other. I don't like her, I don't trust her, and I don't want her anywhere near this investigation."

Roland sighed. "Agreed. I won't speak of it without consulting you first."

Angelica nodded, satisfied.

The waiter breezed to a stop at their table. "Sunny-side up?"

"Ah!" Roland smiled and raised a finger.

The young man set down their plates, and when he was assured that they had everything they needed, he left.

Roland unfurled a napkin and laid it on his lap. "Enough detective work. You have but an hour left in Lake Geneva. Let it be a pleasant one." He raised his water glass.

Angelica smiled in acquiescence and tinked his glass with hers. She knew these last few moments would slip by far too quickly. She already knew she would be coming back—as soon as she felt the boys would be okay without her.

But she also knew, beyond the shadow of a doubt, that she would have to be desperate to work with Monica Steele.

CHAPTER THIRTY-THREE
ANGELICA

———— ✸ ————

They stepped out of the cafe, under a bright red awning. Roland folded up a worn leather wallet and tucked it into his cardigan pocket; he'd insisted on paying.

"Well!" he said cheerily. "Are you ready for the road?"

Angelica tilted her head and watched the water run from the edge of the canopy. She had arrived in Lake Geneva in rain, and she was leaving in rain. And yet her feelings now were so vastly different from what they were then. In ways, no less confused. But somehow, Lake Geneva rain carried with it memories of sunshine. It splashed the sidewalks with echoes of laughter and washed the streets in hope. She had never seen rain like this. She had never been to a place like this.

She didn't want to leave. In the short week she had been here, the lake had somehow burrowed through her skin, become a part of her soul, filled her with its own peculiar light and promise and hope. The sensation was so subtle, it defied description or even notice. She imagined a lifelong resident like Roland never even saw the light peeking out through his own eyes, glowing in the wrinkles of his skin. But it was in him, just as it was now in her. As if

169

the blood in her veins had been replaced with spring-fed lake water, clear as glass, glowing with sun.

The questions were still there. The pain. The betrayal. But she felt almost as if the lake itself promised the wounds would heal. The lake was glad she had come.

She tilted her head and smiled at Roland wanly. "How can I ever thank you?"

"Oh, my dear, don't even mention it." He turned up the collar of his cardigan. The damp air carried the smell of wool with the lanolin still in it, and Angelica noticed a raindrop roll off the sleeve instead of soaking in. "I'm so glad you came," Roland went on. "I can't tell you how deeply I appreciate getting to know you. I'm so glad Fritz found you."

Angelica nodded but could offer no smile.

Roland took her hand in his. "Remember him the way you always knew him. Remember him happy, as I do. There were very few moments in his life when he wasn't truly happy."

Maybe. One day. When she was ready. "You'll let me know as soon as you hear something from your reporter friend?" she asked.

"Of course. Immediately. And you must let me know when you have a reply from the courthouse."

"I will."

"Excellent." His eyebrows lifted. "Oh! I almost forgot. Wait here a moment."

Roland stepped off the sidewalk into the rain and unlocked his car, a black Cadillac SUV with silver trim. He opened the door, took something from the passenger seat, and tucked it under his sweater. Then he jogged back to the awning, shrugging his shoulders against the rain.

"Here," he said, removing a bulky, square item from under his cardigan.

Angelica gasped, recognizing the rich, dark red hue of the padded leather cover. "Your photo album."

He pushed it toward her. "Take it. It's yours."

"But there are so many pictures of Bobby in here."

Roland waved his hand dismissively. "I have millions. My wife was a little camera happy. Please, it would honor me if you had this."

Angelica folded the album to her chest with one arm, then leaned forward and wrapped Roland in a hug with the other. "Thank you," she said, forcing herself to hold back tears.

Roland seemed surprised by her gesture, but quickly settled into the embrace. "You're very welcome." He pulled back. "If you need anything at all, don't hesitate to pick up the phone. And bring those boys of yours to visit sometime. I don't have the catamaran anymore, but we could fire up the old steam yacht. Take them on a grand tour of the lake, the old-fashioned way."

Angelica nodded. "Yes, I will bring the boys. Definitely." Maybe not on her next trip. Not if she was still investigating. But later. One day when she had more answers for her sons. Coming here might prove healing for them.

"Good. Well, then. Have a safe flight."

"I will."

Angelica smiled, then turned and got into her car. Once she'd turned both the ignition and the windshield wipers, she paused to wave, then pulled out into traffic. She drove towards the highway slowly, trying to soak in every last glimpse of the town, the trees, and the lake beyond. Trying to drink a few last drops of the mystic light that lived here. Trying to reconcile it with the darkness that still filled her soul.

Yes. She would be coming back. Soon.

CHAPTER THIRTY-FOUR
MONICA

Angelica Read. The name popped into my head as if it had been on the tip of my tongue since the day I first saw her in Lake Geneva, almost a week ago. My unmarked vehicle moved at a crawl down Main Street through traffic already growing thick for the upcoming weekend, never mind the rain. The petite Hispanic woman with the long, dark hair had embraced Roland Markham, then gotten into a black sedan with Illinois plates and driven away. I was too far away to read the numbers, but it was probably a rental.

What on earth was she doing here? Details of my interview with her in Los Angeles flashed through my mind. She'd sat on her fancy white sofa, looked me in the eye, and swore she'd never heard of Lake Geneva before. That she'd never met her husband's childhood friends, Bobby and Jason. In fact, she denied that Fritz Geissler was her husband at all. She insisted his rightful name was Will Read and that he had been born and raised in Grand Rapids, Michigan.

Then why was she here? Hugging Bobby Markham's father? When I interviewed her at her home, my conclusion was that she had been as deceived as anyone about her husband's identity and background. But was she?

I slipped into her parking spot and hopped out of the SUV. Roland was still standing under the awning outside Egg Harbor, hands in his cardigan pockets as he watched Angelica drive away.

"Hey, Roland." Rain tapped against my black weatherproof jacket with the embroidered badge on the left breast.

"Monica." Roland grinned, straightening as he saw me. "How are you this fine, wet day?"

I stepped next to him under the protection of the canopy and nodded at the retreating black sedan. "Wasn't that Angelica Read?" I pushed my hands into my pockets to keep them warm.

"Why, yes. She mentioned you two had met."

"How do you know her?"

"We bumped into each other at the library. Struck up a conversation and found out we had... well, that we had common connections."

I shifted an eyebrow. They'd just happened to meet... at the library? Then again, what were the alternatives? That she and Roland had known each other all along? If that were the case, how? She'd married Fritz years after he vanished. If Roland knew her, then he'd known where Fritz was—and never told me. The initial investigation had cleared him of any involvement in the Markham Ring—I'd double checked every detail personally.

The next possibility was that Angelica had sought Roland out on purpose. I remembered her tears and shouts during our interview. She'd been the inconsolable, terrified, disbelieving wife—not buying for a minute that her husband was a fugitive living under a false identity.

But did I buy that? How could a woman be married to a guy for fifteen years and have no idea who he really was?

"She's a long way from LA," I commented.

"Yes." Roland shrugged. "Well, you can understand, I'm sure. Her husband's death, the truth of his past—such a shock. She came to see the place where he grew up."

"Why?" I asked, perhaps too bluntly.

Roland looked at me, befuddled, offended even. "To get to know him. Granted, most people square that away during the dating phase, but not every couple is that traditional."

I couldn't help grinning acknowledgment of his witty and annoyed comeback. I nodded my chin in the direction Angelica had driven. "Looks like you two hit it off."

"Yes. We had many memories to exchange."

"What did you tell her?"

Roland's sky-blue eyes turned a little harder. "Everything I could," he said firmly. "She has a right to know, don't you agree?"

I decided to try to cool the conversation down. "Sure, yeah," I said with a generous shrug. But was it really a coincidence that she'd managed to find Roland Markham, one of the few people in Lake Geneva who had known all three members of the Markham Ring intimately? What did she want from him?

"You're upset with me, aren't you?" Roland went on. "You think I've told her too much."

"I didn't say that."

"But you thought it. Tell me, Monica, does solving crime mean we must all cease to be decent people? She lost her husband."

I sighed. I hadn't wanted this to turn into an argument. "I just want you to stay safe," I said. "I don't know much about Angelica Read—"

He pointed across the street. "You don't know much about that woman, either, I'll wager." He'd indicated a random shopper with paper boutique bags in her hand and an umbrella over her shoulder.

174

Heat rose to my face, despite the cold in the air. His point was irrelevant. "Angelica was directly connected to one of the members of the Markham Ring—a member whose murder is still unsolved." I motioned toward the lake. "We found his body at the end of *your* pier. Did you tell her that?"

Roland met my gaze and nodded soberly. "Yes, I did." In the tense silence that followed, the raindrops drummed on the awning. "You believe she's a suspect?"

"At the least, she's a witness who has proved very uncooperative."

"Well. I won't interfere with your job. Mistrust is the price you paid, I suppose, when you donned the badge." He lifted his thin white eyebrows. "Lucky for me, I never took any such oaths of office. Which means I can blithely go on treating her like any decent human being—one who just lost her husband violently and tragically."

I wasn't sure if his naivety made me love him or hate him. I sighed. "Promise me you'll be careful."

He grinned. "If I had a dollar for every time you told me to be careful, I'd be a rich man."

I scoffed. "You *are* a rich man. But you'll be a *dead* rich man if you don't start taking that promise more seriously."

"Well." Roland smiled. "I can think of a number of charities that will be delighted to finally receive my estate."

I groaned and turned away. My conversations with him made me feel as if I were running in a hamster wheel. I felt his hand on my arm and looked at him again.

"I don't mean to distress you, Monica. I'm sorry."

Well, that was something anyway. I sighed. "Will you let me know if Angelica does or says anything strange?"

He hesitated, mouth open as if he wanted to speak but thought better of it.

I frowned. "Roland, what do you know? What has she said to you?"

175

He groaned. "I really do think the two of you need to sit down and have a good talk sometime."

"We already had a talk."

"It wasn't a very good one."

"Well, don't worry. I have every intention of talking to her again."

"All she wants is to know who killed her husband and why."

"I'll notify her as soon as we have information."

Roland looked away and rocked on the balls of his feet. "Unless she notifies you first," he muttered absently.

"What's that?" His meaning clicked into place. "She's investigating her husband's death?"

Roland looked momentarily guilty, as if he'd said something he wasn't supposed to. But immediately afterwards, he turned defensive. "Well, can you blame her? It's been three weeks without a scrap of information. The girl is starving for answers."

"Has she found anything?"

"No. Of course not. You know best that clues to this case aren't exactly littering the ground."

I nodded, feeling justified. "But you'll tell me if she finds anything?"

"As I've already said, the two of you ought to sit down and have a good talk."

"Work with her?"

"Well, yes. Why not?"

"She's not law enforcement."

"And she wasn't born yesterday, either. I think you're missing an opportunity."

"Duly noted. In the meantime, you'll at least tell me if she says or does anything strange?"

He scoffed. "I hardly think—"

I hardened my gaze. "Roland, I'm about to investigate the very real possibility that Angelica Read knew exactly who her husband was and what he did. I don't know how

176

deeply involved she could be or what her goals and motives are. And so I want to know why she came here and why she's talking to *you,* someone who knew Bobby, Fritz, and Jason closely. She could be playing you for information."

His brow went stormy—an expression I'd never seen on him before. "I've told you why she came."

"And I'll accept that—for now. In the meantime, please, *please* be careful."

"I promise," he said, underscoring his words with a lift of his shoulders. "If Angelica does or says anything strange, you will be the first to know."

"Good." I pulled the car keys out of my pocket and stepped back into the rain. "Stay safe," I said, pointing a finger at him.

"Duly noted," he said, throwing my own words back at me.

I wagged my head and got back into the SUV. There was no helping Roland Markham, and it annoyed the piss out of me.

CHAPTER THIRTY-FIVE
ROLAND

———— ⚓ ————

Roland watched Monica drive away and sighed, squeezing his hands into fists inside his pockets. Well. He'd already gone back on his promise to Angelica not to mention her investigation. No doubt she'd be furious. Still, he had said nothing about her primary theory: that Wade Erickson was a member of the Markham Ring. And besides, he'd stood by his convictions; Monica and Angelica *should* speak to each other, and not in an interrogation. Then Angelica could air her beliefs herself.

Meanwhile, Angelica had given him work to do. He pulled his phone out of his pocket, stared at it, and sighed. May as well get the hardest task out of the way first.

He found Tommy Thomlin in his contacts and pressed his number.

CHAPTER THIRTY-SIX
TOMMY

———— ✹ ————

My phone rang just as I was rolling up the TheraBands my physical therapist had given me. She'd taught me a number of exercises I could do while seated, and as such, I was taking up a well-cushioned recliner in the living room, listening to the radio while I worked on max reps. So far, I could do all of five without a break. Regardless of my prowess, Nancy was impressed by my self-motivation. They say all you need is the right reason—and Bailey was as strong a reason as they come.

I reached for my phone, half wondering if it could possibly be Bailey, finally returning my call.

It wasn't. The screen said Roland Markham.

I frowned. We barely talked these days unless it had to do with his mail. He generally preferred to call me directly, rather than the cruise line office. But he could read the barometer and knew where my loyalty lay. Much as I hated choosing between my two oldest friends, Wade had been right to take a firm stance with Bobby when Roland couldn't. Still, I'd always felt like a middle child, trapped between siblings and wishing there were a way to keep the peace.

179

I picked up. "Well, hello, Roland. How are you?"

"I'm fine, Tommy, fine. The better question is, how are you? You sound well."

"Oh, I'm staying pretty snug." I avoided mentioning that I was at Wade's house. In addition to being instructed against doing so, I felt no need to open old wounds between Roland and Wade.

"I was shocked when I heard the news. I'm so sorry."

I tried to formulate a response and realized I didn't know what to say. There was no etiquette surrounding how to talk about an attempt on your life.

No. He'd never meant to kill me. He'd said so himself. I frowned as fleeting memories teased at the edge of conscious thought. What he'd wanted was to *play* with my life.

My gaze slowly fixated on the radio. My mind tumbled down a long, black tunnel. At the other end was another place. Another voice. I found words that were seared into my memory without my even knowing.

"There's no fun in killin', did'ya know that? I kill you, it's over. But this way?" He smirked. "You'll never be the same man again, Tommy. I promise you that."

"Tommy? Hello? Are you there?"

Roland's voice chased me down the tunnel. Nagged at the corners of my awareness. Introduced discord into my reality. Shattered the images playing before me. It wasn't real. I was pulled back up the tunnel, moving faster and faster, until I emerged again in the recliner in Wade's living room, staring at the radio.

I shook my head, confused, trying to grasp what was real and suddenly realizing I was talking to Roland. "I'm sorry, what did you say?" How long had I checked out?

"I was just asking, is it true that you're staying at Wade's house?"

180

Well. The secret was out, then. My heart sank. How common was that knowledge? "Where'd you hear that?" I knew better than to outright admit it.

"Oh, I had it from Brian. He said that's where Robb Landis was forwarding all the cards and flowers that were showing up at the cruise line office."

Well, that was that. If Brian knew, then everyone knew. He was too affable and simple-minded to realize that he shouldn't spread that information. I'd have to tell Wade that my whereabouts were no longer a secret.

"I was just curious," Roland went on, "I don't suppose you've noticed anything... unusual while you've been at Wade's?"

"What do you mean?"

"Oh, I don't know. Everyone's behaving normally? I mean—they're treating you well?"

Behaving normally? What was that supposed to mean? The question was so odd, I asked myself again whether I was experiencing the real world or lost in some other daydream.

Still, it made the most sense to continue the conversation. I eyed the stack of books, glass of water, and plate of healthy snacks Nancy had left within arm's reach of the recliner. "I haven't been so coddled since I was six months old."

"Oh, really? And you're allowed to go out, of course?"

"I'm sure I would be, if I could cross a room on my own."

"Ah. I see." He sounded disappointed, like someone who hadn't gotten the answer he wanted.

Why was the conversation so bizarre? "Roland, what's this all about?"

He groaned under his breath. "It's nothing, Tommy. I'm sure of it. You see, a friend of mine—well, we were examining the facts at hand and there's a remote possibility..." He trailed off.

181

"Spit it out." We were both too old to dally around like this.

Roland sighed. "There's talk of a fourth member of Bobby's old ring. Our sons are gone, Tommy. Who else could be cleaning house?"

Cleaning house. The words left in blood on both my window and Roland's. My retribution had already come for me but failed.

No, that made no sense. *There's no fun in killin'.* If the man who shot me was some fourth member of the Markham Ring bent on cleaning house, why was I still alive? Why did he spare me?

To toy with me. That's what he'd said. Why did he want to toy with me?

I stared at the vivid memories, lost at the end of the black tunnel. Screwing up my courage, I stepped into the darkness. Reached out. Pushed against the memories, trying to touch them, to see them clearly. But the images resisted, like frosted glass. Now that I wanted them, they wouldn't come. But I knew there was a reason why my assailant had attacked me. He'd *told* me the reason. What was it...?

"Whoever this fourth member is, he's shown a keen interest in anyone even remotely connected to the old gang—even next of kin."

I stared at the blurred memories. A keen interest, yes, hence the warnings drawn in blood. But the fourth member hadn't acted on his threats. Roland was alive. I'd been attacked by someone else, so far as I could tell. Why hadn't the fourth member acted on his threats? Why had I instead been left to the mercy of some other lunatic with some other agenda? *What was that agenda?*

And then the frosted glass cracked. Vanished. But the scene I saw wasn't the assailant kneeling over me. I saw my son Jason. Alive. Our last conversation as we stood in

182

darkness in my own backyard. I didn't know it then, but it was mere hours before he was murdered.

"I gotta tell you something. I don't have much time…"

The words played through my mind, but I glanced around me. The recliner was real. The side table was real. The phone still pressed to my ear was real. This wasn't a flashback. I was in control of this moment. I allowed myself to explore the memory. There were answers here. Answers I needed to know.

I remembered his pleading tone. But I'd been furious with him and his every life choice, from allowing himself to be dragged into Bobby's schemes, to murdering a cop to save his own skin. Worst of all, I was livid that he had gotten his girlfriend pregnant and then abandoned both of them without so much as knowing about the child. That child was my mail jumper, Bailey, and she was doing her best to survive in an abusive home.

"Please, you don't know what's coming," Jason pleaded.

But *he* had. Somehow, he had known everything—who the fourth member was and what he wanted—but in my pride and self-righteousness, I hadn't let him get a word in edgewise. The next thing I knew, he was dead.

And I knew who had killed him.

I turned to another pane of opaque glass. A memory I was hesitant to trigger. But there were answers. I needed them. I touched the glass, and it shattered.

I breathed. Fought against the pain. Struggled to keep my mind clear. "You killed my son." It wasn't a question.

The head bobbed, the sunlight from behind blurring all his features. "He went down blazin'," the man assured me.

"Why did you kill my son?"

He shrugged. "Money."

Squaring my jaw, I stroked the leather arms of the recliner. Felt the seams and the stitches. The cracked, supple edges, worn by use. I was still here. I was still in control. I kept asking questions.

Had the man who shot me simply lied to torture me more? Or was it true? Was he in fact related to the Markham Ring? Was he the fourth member? If so, who hired him to kill Jason? Why? And why did he shoot me? Shoot me, but not kill me?

"Tommy," Roland went on.

His voice didn't have as far to tug me this time. I had avoided drowning in the memories. They didn't dominate my mind, controlling me like a rogue sailor hauling lines he shouldn't. I was the captain now. Why wasn't I always? How did I have the bars stripped from my shoulders sometimes? The helm pried from my hands?

"Tommy," Roland went on, "have you ever considered that..." He sighed heavily. "Well, that Wade could be the fourth member of the ring?"

His words brought my swirling thoughts to a screeching halt. The entire ship crashed on rocks neither I nor the rogue sailor had known were there.

Wade? I repeated, incredulous.

"Well, yes. Consider it—"

But I couldn't. Not even for a moment. "Wade wouldn't kill my son."

Roland paused. What he said next, he said flatly but tinged with anger. "He killed mine."

The hull scraped harder against the rocks. What was happening? What was this conversation anymore? "It's not the same," I blurted. "That was self-defense, Roland. He had no choice." I knew immediately it was the wrong thing to say.

His voice was cold. "Yes. I've heard his story."

"Story? You think he lied?"

"I'm merely saying he had room to do so, if he chose."

I shook my head. This was insanity. Maybe I shouldn't have left Roland to himself for so long. I couldn't begrudge him his anger, nor for directing it at Wade. But was this what he was doing all alone in that big house? Concocting wild theories?

"I'm merely suggesting there are oddities," Roland went on. "For instance, what drew Wade's attention to those burglaries in the first place? They had nothing to do with Lake Geneva. And then what would induce the boys to target a bank *here,* of all places? Conveniently in *Wade's* jurisdiction?"

Did Roland really not know the answers? "The burglaries drew Wade's attention because they had Bobby's personality all over them. And Bobby chose a bank in Lake Geneva because he was cocky and wanted to pull one over on his own hometown. Wade caught him in the act because he knew Bobby was in town and he knew by then what to look for. Wade told me everything. Everything he was free to talk about, at least."

"I understand," said Roland. "You don't believe me. Frankly, I'm not sure I believe me, either. The only reason I mention it is because—well, I'm worried. You're there. In his house. And if there were a remote possibility the theory were true, I wouldn't count myself any kind of friend if I said nothing."

"If your theory is true, then Wade not only murdered my son; he had me shot, too. And now he's putting me up while I recover? What would be the point?"

"You don't have to believe me. I only want you to keep your eyes open. You should be careful."

"And you? I hear Monica Steele's got her hands full trying to get you to take your own security more seriously. Your bank balance isn't going to leap between you and a bullet, Roland."

He was silent, and I realized I'd utterly failed at stopping while I was ahead. In all the long years we'd known each other, the vast disparity in our financial situations had never been an issue. I had truly never cared that his checkbook could lap mine twenty times. If anything, I'd pitied him when we were boys. He was growing up alone and unloved in that vast mansion while his parents dallied in society and finance. So why was I rubbing his wealth in his face now? Was I that upset he suspected Wade?

"Should you ever find that I'm right," he said, "I recommend you say something to Monica. Nothing leapt between *you* and a bullet, either."

He hung up.

I sighed and slapped my phone down on the side table.

The kitchen door opened. Nancy's voice called from the kitchen. "Tommy! Ready for PT?"

PT? It couldn't be that time already.

But then the mantle clock, a stately antique that had been in Nancy's family for generations, groaned to life and struck the hour.

CHAPTER THIRTY-SEVEN
ROLAND

Roland paced beneath the awning in front of Egg Harbor, fuming. What was wrong with this town? Monica was convinced a mourning widow could be a murder suspect, and Tommy couldn't fathom Wade killing his son.

Well, Roland could picture it just fine. As clearly as if he'd stood in that alley, watching as Wade pulled the trigger and the light left Bobby's eyes.

He had been surprised at just how vehemently he'd defended Angelica's argument. The theory was based on nothing but conjecture and suspicion, with literally nothing to back it up. Well, perhaps Tommy's naivety had pushed him beyond the point of resistance. After all, why was Tommy's son more special than his?

CHAPTER THIRTY-EIGHT
BUD

———— ⚓ ————

Rain was lousy for business. The morning's mist had turned to a regular downpour, and no one was coming into the bar besides a handful of the boys. They sat on stools drinking beer, chewing the fat, and half-interestedly watching a replay of last Sunday's ball game. Bud polished his taps, running a soft chamois into every nook. There were few things more beautiful than a gleaming row of stainless steel taps. He'd cleaned the bar, too, rubbing in the polish until the wood glowed. The chips in the finish only added character, as did the stickers from various beer companies. He loved that bar. Just wished he were serving more drinks on it right now...

The bell above the door chimed, and Bud looked to the front room. Skull crossed the threshold, his Guns N' Roses tee shirt speckled with rain and his spiked hair damp. He looked tired and sorely in need of a drink.

"Well, looky, looky!" said Tony, a wiry kid who could stride confidently in any direction with any number of feet stuffed into his mouth. "Where the hell you been, Skull?"

He slid onto a stool and rested his arms on the bar, the rose-and-skull tattoo he was known for in plain view on the back of his forearm. It was a gorgeous bit of work. Bud never let on he was jealous.

"My aunt was sick. Had to head out of town." Skull nodded to Bud by way of greeting. "The usual."

Bud pulled a pint glass from the shelf and filled it with Pilsner, eying Skull through slitted eyes. The guy didn't have an aunt...

Tony didn't know that. "Sorry to hear it, man. Hope she's doing better."

Skull nodded. "She is, she is. Thanks." He nodded to the TV screen. "I missed that game. Who won?"

"Oh, my God. We creamed 'em. It's almost painful to watch, man."

"That bad, huh?"

"Eleven to two, Brewers."

"Ouch."

"I dunno," said Steve, a slouchy kid with a dopey face who somehow reminded Bud of Kung Fu Panda. "Cardinals still have a shot at Central."

Tony scowled at him. "How you figure that?"

While Steve and Tony argued the fate of the season, Bud slid the beer across the bar to Skull. He nodded his thanks and took a thirsty pull. Sometimes when Skull was busy at work, he didn't even have the chance to stop for a drink.

Bud leaned on the bar, turning his shoulder to the others. "So, where were you really?" He spoke low so no one but Skull would hear. "You told me you had five uncles, and not a girl out of the whole lot."

Skull stared past him to the TV. "I could have been talking about my mother's side."

"But you weren't, were you?"

Skull took another drink, saying nothing.

"Where were you?" said Bud.

"I had a job."

"For who?" Skull only had one line of work, and the people who paid him paid dearly. Though to anyone who

asked, he was a contractor who built agricultural sites—
feedlots and the like. But he was never taking new clients.
His schedule was full, but thanks for asking. That is, unless
you needed the co-owner of the feedlot shadowed and his
every secret revealed, business or personal. Then Skull had
an opening. An opening that more often than not ended in
the subject of his investigation turning up dead. But the
dirty work was never Skull's job. Sometimes it was Bud's.

Skull remained silent, and that made Bud hot under the
collar. Granted, in their line of work, you didn't drop names
unless there was a reason. But if this was a simple case of
client confidentiality, why didn't Skull just say so and tell
Bud to buzz off? Why was he being so cagey?

"You're not working for The Man still, are you?"

Skull sipped his beer. His lack of response was
admission enough for Bud.

Bud leaned back but kept his voice low. The rest of the
guys were having an animated discussion about baseball,
anyway. "Aw, c'mon, how could you do that? How can you
sit there drinking *my* beer and tell me you're still working
for him?"

"You and I were contracted independently. When you
went outside the bounds of your agreement and closed
down an entity The Man never specified, your contract was
canceled."

Closed down? He meant shooting Tommy Thomlin.
Well, the bastard deserved it. He'd told the cops that Bailey
had a black eye. Tried to get her taken away from him. Bud
spread his hands. "I'm a freelancer. I can work my own
gigs."

"Not when it interferes with a contract. It's all about
making the customer happy, remember Bud?" Skull tilted
his head and lifted his glass in a toast.

Bud leaned in and tapped the counter. "He tried to have
me..." He struggled to come up with the metaphors as
gracefully as Skull did. "Terminated. Don't you know that?

190

He sicced JB on me—" he jabbed his thumb to the dish room where Jimmy Beacon used to work "—with a freakin' bomb!" He was out of metaphors—and patience. This game was stupid, anyway. "Firing me is one thing. But tryin' to blow my ass to bits? What the hell?"

Tony looked back over his shoulder. He'd heard Bud's tense tone and had a look of curiosity on his face.

Skull set the mug down and stood abruptly. "Come 'ere."

"What?"

He beckoned vigorously, making his way toward the end of the bar. "Come 'ere, come 'ere, come 'ere. C'mon."

Bud glanced at Tony and Steve. They were both staring now. Bud followed Skull. Skull grabbed him by the elbow and steered him inside the walk-in liquor cabinet behind the bar. He closed the door behind them, then whirled on Bud. Bud braced. If Skull threw him a punch in here amongst all his best liquors...

But Skull merely braced his feet and squared up to Bud. His voice was low but tense. Bud could still hear the bar music above it. "These aren't games we're playing. You know too much. You're a liability to The Man now."

Bud jabbed a finger in Skull's face. "Well, too frickin' bad. He shoulda known better than to piss me off. Calling a hit on his hit man? No way. No one's ever put a tail on me, no one's ever got the drop on me, and no one's ever had a hit on me. You got that? The Man's in deep shit now, and he's gonna pay."

Skull glared at him. "What are you saying?"

"There are two things I'm good at—cookin' and killin'. And he ain't gettin' my cookin'. You can tell him I said that, Mister Info Man." He pushed past Skull and grabbed the door handle.

"You're playing with fire, Bud."

"I'm a chef. It's my job." He swung the door open and waved his hand. "Now get out of my liquor cabinet. In fact, you can get out of my bar."

Skull glared at him, then brushed past and didn't stop until he was out the front door.

Bud didn't even care if Skull warned The Man. Once Bud decided someone was going to die…

They died.

His mind was made up.

CHAPTER THIRTY-NINE
TOMMY

———— ✾ ————

The day's rain had built to a gale by the time Nancy put dinner on the table. Since I'd been here, she and I had eaten alone every night. Apparently Wade hadn't managed to keep regular hours since the day Fritz Geissler was murdered. Nancy simply kept his dinner warm until he was able to put in an appearance.

She was scrubbing the dishes and I was in my chair in the living room, feet up with a book in my lap, when the kitchen door opened. Nancy and Wade's hellos were followed by an embrace, their nightly ritual, no matter how late. I tried not to think of my Laina, gone these fifteen years. The empty ache was still there.

Instead, I thought of my conversation with Roland. When I considered how tender and affectionate Wade was with his wife, his children, his grandkids—I felt fully justified in believing that Roland was insane. He couldn't face the fact of what his son had become—not just a thief, but a man willing to draw a gun on an old friend. And yet I understood Roland's incredulity. I still couldn't believe my own son had aligned himself with Bobby's madness.

Nancy's voice carried from the kitchen, despite keeping her tone to barely a whisper. "I think you should talk to Tommy."

"Oh?"

"There's something on his mind. I can tell."

"Okay."

"I'll fix you a plate."

"Thanks."

They kissed. Wade moved into the living room. With a scratchy rip, he pulled apart the Velcro of his duty belt. His rank gave him the privilege of dressing in office attire, but he generally opted for the uniform. Showing solidarity for the rank and file of the department was important to him. He never wanted to forget the countless hours he'd put in behind the wheel of a cruiser or what it was like being out on the street.

"Good book, Tommy?" he asked. Like every night, he blocked my view of his sidearm with his body, then slipped into his office where he kept his gun safe. I tried not to shake my head at him. I liked to think I could handle the sight of a gun. He and Nancy were going to exhaust themselves with their never-ending coddling.

I eyed my place in the book—a collection of biographies of Wisconsinites who had fought in World War II—and found I'd read the entire book in a day. "Nancy might have to make another run to the library. I'm almost through the stack she brought me."

Wade returned to the living room, removing his tie and loosening the collar of his shirt. "You're going to run out of Wisconsin history. Might have to cross over to Illinois."

"Never."

He laughed. Wisconsin's opinion of being overrun by weekenders from Illinois was infamous. But I was only being obstinate for the sake of the joke. I'd read plenty of histories of Illinois. Lake Geneva's history was so closely linked with the Windy City, it couldn't exactly be avoided.

Wade hiked up his pant legs and dropped into a nearby easy chair. "Nancy thought you had something on your mind today."

"I did. I was only waiting for you to get home to tell you about it."

"Oh, good. I was afraid I'd have to bring out the thumb screws."

I ignored Wade's lousy humor. It was a thin cover. Clearly, he thought it was his duty to nourish my mental health as well as my physical health. I couldn't wait to get back to my own house and my own routines.

Though I'd prefer if the guy who shot me was captured, first.

I looked at Wade significantly. "It's not a secret anymore that I'm here."

The lighthearted humor faded from his eyes. His businesslike cop face pushed through, an expression I was familiar with. He needed to hear details.

"I had a call from Roland today. He knew where I was. He had it from Brian Meissner, my replacement driver. If Brian knows, the whole lake knows."

Wade's brow furrowed. If he wasn't already keeping a gun by his bed, he would now.

A moment later, he wiped away his concern, sat up straight, and rolled his shoulders. "All right. Good to know." And that was all. Again, he was trying to protect me from worrying. Anyway, it wasn't like there was a lot more he could do. He already had an alarm system. And unless I'd missed my guess, he already had extra patrols going past the house. I couldn't remember that many police cars slow-cruising down this street during a normal summer. I just hoped he wouldn't ask Nancy to stay home from work to guard me. I didn't think I could swallow that many bowls of chicken noodle soup in a day.

The microwave beeped in the kitchen. Nancy peeked around the corner, wiping a glass with a tea towel. "Sweetheart, your dinner's ready."

Wade rose and moved toward the kitchen. *Should I say anything about the rest of my conversation with Roland? About his suspicions of Wade? It was such insanity...*

Nancy looked at me. "Tommy, I made peach cobbler. Want any?"

I shook my head. But the more I thought about it, the more I felt I should tell Wade everything. This was no time to keep him in the dark.

"Wade?"

"Yes?" he stopped where the carpet turned to tile.

"There's something else Roland said."

"Yeah?" He rested his hands on his hips and shifted his weight to one foot.

I paused. Now that it came down to it, how did you even say such a thing out loud? *Our old friend is convinced you're a serial killer.*

"I think he's going a little batty in that old house of his," I said.

"How so?"

"He thinks..." I thumbed the book, struggling one more time with how to say it. I finally just let it spill. "He thinks you're some kind of fourth member of the Markham Ring." When Wade failed to react, as if my words hadn't registered, I made it more blatant. "He thinks you killed Fritz. He thinks you killed Jason."

Nancy's mouth dropped open. The glass fell from her hand and shattered on the floor.

Wade only continued to stare, his face unreadable. I wasn't sure if he was angry at Roland...

Or me.

CHAPTER FORTY
BUD

———————— ⎈ ————————

Bud poured more whiskey into his shot glass, his hand unsteady, some of the amber liquid sloshing over the side. Leaning over unsteadily, he slammed the half-empty bottle into a pile of magazines on his living room coffee table. Then he threw back the shot. The alcohol burned down his throat, setting every muscle fiber on fire.

He stared into the TV and the sitcom showing stupid people living stupid lives. When the audience laughed, he raged. What was so funny? *What was so funny?* Why were they laughing at him? The faces on the screen morphed into the faces of his past. Pointing. Laughing. Calling him names. He was too fat. Too ugly. Too dumb. Too klutzy. And that wasn't even the worst of it. Cold rage poured through his veins. He flexed his fingers. Instead of cold glass, he felt the cold skin of his first victim.

She was so tiny. So innocent. Amelia Beacon. What had possessed him? The need to make someone else feel the numb, cold hurt that he felt. The desire had been there for so long. He was done tamping the rage down. Keeping it bottled up.

He hadn't meant to kill her. But the girl's screams had turned to sobs, and then her sobs had gone cold quiet. He had the chance to stop, and he didn't. He just kept going. He remembered looking down at the cold, dead body and feeling the icy cold fear of knowing he was a murderer. He'd ditched her body. He'd run. He'd hid. He'd waited. And after months and months went by without a single tail put on him, he felt the confident, cold certainty that no one would ever catch him. That he was invincible.

That he could kill whenever he wanted.

And kill, he did. Again and again and again…

He wiped his mouth with the back of his hand. "No one kills a killer," he muttered to the idiots on the TV screen. "No one puts a hit on the hit man."

CHAPTER FORTY-ONE
SKULL

———— ✿ ————

Skull stepped into his bedroom, his shoes silent on the plush white carpet. The recessed lights were dimmed, and he left them that way. He set his phone on the black walnut vanity and pressed the home button.

"Siri, play strings."

Siri chirped pleasantly and began to play soft violins, piano, and guitar. Skull breathed deeply, allowing the stress to flow off him. Tonight was the first time he'd ever been kicked out of a bar. He wasn't shocked it was Bud's bar. Bud Weber was ruled by his emotions. In the dangerous game he played, he trusted his success—his life—to luck.

Skull wasn't sure why The Man had hired Weber in the first place. But then again, raw emotions were The Man's plaything. He molded and twisted them however he saw fit. It was art. Skull had never seen his own clandestinely-acquired information fed into such a breathtaking symphony before. So many melodies. So many counterpoints. His other clients were cave men by comparison. It was a pleasure working for The Man. Watching him at his art.

Of course, Bud was too simple to appreciate something like that. And too dumb to value his own hide. Maybe he thought his services invaluable. How would The Man finish all his plans without a hit man?

But didn't Bud see? There was no need for a hit man. The Man Upstairs could manipulate the most ordinary of souls into doing the unthinkable. He'd pushed Jimmy Beacon, a lonely teenage boy, into killing innocent people in his thirst for revenge. Everyone had a breaking point. It was merely a matter of finding that wound and leaning into it until the subject snapped.

If Bud wasn't careful, he'd make himself The Man's next object of affection. Skull didn't even consider *himself* above The Man's notice. This was definitely a client to keep happy.

He pulled his tee shirt over his head and stared into the mirror. Thorny vines embraced the *roseschadel,* cradling the cracked skull like a lost loved one. From there, they twisted up his arm, transforming into flowing wind across his shoulder, turning into a stampede of horses across his chest. From there, the ink gathered into billowing thunderheads on his right bicep, slashing his arm with lightning and rain. Hidden in the clouds was the image of a weeping woman.

He'd already lived a long life. He already had a long story to tell—though he'd never told it. Instead, he'd gone under the needle and bought a lot of ink. His right forearm was still blank. He didn't know yet what would go there. He dreamed of a glorious sunset, breaking through the clouds of the thunderstorm.

Other times he saw knives. Daggers. Blood dripping off the points and running down his fingers.

Only a handful of women had ever seen his ink in its full glory. They asked him what it meant. But Skull wasn't in the business of giving up his own information. He diverted their questions with a warning look, followed by a tantalizing kiss and a night of ever-spiraling passion. After all, a man of secrets was alluring. He knew girls in many cities, wherever his jobs took him. But none of them provided what he had lost. He didn't ask them to. Only to help him forget.

When he thought about it, the daggers were far more likely than the sunset.

The violins stopped, interrupted by his phone vibrating softly. Skull glanced at the screen. It brought up a string of numbers he'd committed to memory. He picked up his phone. His business hours were whenever his clients needed him.

"Yes?"

The Man's voice crooned low, calm, in control, like it always was. "Are you available tonight?"

Angelica Read was back in Los Angeles, so she wasn't the subject, unless The Man wanted him to explore her digital life. But then why the late-night call? No, in all likelihood, there was a new target. But who? Skull was eager to find out. To see the next melody line in The Man's symphony come to the forefront.

"What do you need to know?"

"Things are maturing nicely," said The Man. There was satisfaction in his voice, and Skull took that as a personal compliment. "I think it's time to start Phase B."

Skull smiled. "I'll do it tonight."

"Excellent. I look forward to hearing from you."

"Yes, sir."

The Man hung up. The violins played again. Skull set his phone down. Studied the thunderhead and the weeping woman in the mirror.

Phase B. Things were about to get interesting. This town hadn't seen anything yet.

He opened a drawer, found a plain black hoodie, and pulled it on over his head. He dug deeper into the drawer, found his 9mm, and popped in a clip.

Killing wasn't his department. But for The Man, he might even consider it.

CHAPTER FORTY-TWO
TOMMY

———————— ✵ ————————

The mantle clock struck once.

My eyes fluttered open. I was still in the recliner in the living room. I must have fallen asleep during the ten o'clock news. A quilt lay over me, a fresh glass of water sat on the end table, and my phone was plugged in to charge—all Nancy's doing, no doubt.

After she'd dropped the glass earlier, she'd apologized and cleaned up, chattering about poor Roland and how terrible it must be to live alone in that vast house.

Wade had passed wordlessly into the kitchen to eat his dinner, and never commented. Well, the man was exhausted. I'm sure being accused of murder—when finding the murderer consumed his every waking moment—was the last thing he needed.

And so the rest of the evening had passed in awkward silence.

I looked to the mantle clock. Half past eleven. What had woken me up? I didn't think it was the clock itself. Granted, I hadn't been sleeping very deeply lately. My subconscious seemed determined to keep one eye open.

I scanned the room, my eyes traveling between the pools of darkness in the room and the windows overlooking the street. There were plenty of shadows for my imagination to play in. But nothing moved. My gaze shifted to the spindled oak railing, the hardwood stairs down to the split-level foyer, and the front door. It had no window, but the sidelights glowed softly, illuminated by the streetlights beyond. The swirled stained glass muted the view of the small front porch and the yard beyond.

I made out the shadow of a man crouching by the door.

My heart leapt into my throat. A voice rang through my ears.

"IF you live, I'll see you later. But I promise you this: YOU won't see ME."

A hand touched my shoulder. I startled so hard, I nearly shouted. Wade appeared from behind my recliner. My eyes went to the gun in his hand and my heart nearly stopped beating.

But his eyes were focused across the room. I followed his gaze to the door.

The shadow was gone. I frowned. Had I only imagined it?

"Stay here," Wade whispered. As if I were capable of going far on my own.

Without a sound, he moved to the door, turned the lock, and slipped outside. I was relieved to hear the lock snick shut behind him. His shadow passed the sidelight, then vanished.

I strained my ears, not sure what I was expecting—a shout, a scuffle, Wade's gun going off. But minutes dragged by, and all I heard was the beating of my own heart and the ticking of the mantle clock.

CHAPTER FORTY-THREE
ROLAND

❈

Roland turned a yellowed page in *Anna Karénina,* the original 1887 translation. Gold light pooled on the page from the lamp behind his armchair. He never stayed up so late, but sleep eluded him. The day's drizzle had built to a storm, then broke. Billowing clouds scurried toward the far shore, carrying their wrath elsewhere but leaving behind erratic bursts of wind and flashes of lightning. Meanwhile, his mind still roiled over his conversation with Tommy earlier in the day. Even Angelica's text, reporting that she'd landed safely in Los Angeles, had failed to lift his spirits.

He hadn't spoken to his friend yet, the reporter. But he would. He felt a little more determined now to follow up on Angelica's suspicions.

Metal clinked on stone.

Roland looked up at the French doors but only saw the reflection of a floor lamp, a wingback chair, and an old man reading a book. Something must have been knocked loose by the gale and fallen, but for a moment he couldn't think what it may be. Then he remembered that he had been re-potting the flowers in the cornice pieces the other day. Had he remembered to put away the hand trowel, or was it still lying on the stone railing, the last place he could remember seeing it? The wind might have slid it toward the edge.

He considered getting up to put it away. But it was dark and unpleasant out, and he had arrived at one of his favorite chapters. He settled deeper into his armchair. The trowel could wait for the morning, provided he remembered.

Two pages later, an uncomfortable sensation crept up his back. That feeling that someone is looking at you.

Knowing he was being ridiculous—hoping he was—Roland looked again to the doors. Old as they were, the wood was softened, chipped in places despite countless layers of new paint, and the panes remained speckled with age, even with a maid coming 'round every week to clean. The grandfather clock ticked the seconds ponderously. Was it his imagination, or was that the shadowy outline of a man beyond the glass?

Roland closed his book and raised his voice, knowing it would carry. "Who's there?"

The silence that followed could have proved Roland a madman, talking to an empty room, accusing his grandfather clock of breaking and entering.

Roland laid *Anna* on the side table, rose, and faced the doors. The waves churned against the shore and thunder rolled in the distance. Through his own shadowy reflection, Roland caught a glimmer of light, as if streaming down the barrel of a gun held low.

Every muscle tensing, Roland stared boldly where he knew the eyes must be. "Come into the light."

As if by answer, lightning flashed, illuminating the silhouette of a tall man dressed in black, a gun in his hand.

The man raised his arm, then brought the butt of the gun down hard on the glass and the fragile wooden frames. They exploded. Roland threw up his hands as the shards flew toward him.

206

CHAPTER FORTY-FOUR
BUD

It hadn't gone right. Nothing had gone right. The Man was still alive. How was The Man still alive?

Bud ran through the woods, rain soaking his tee shirt and jeans, tears soaking his face. Branches ripped at his cheeks and arms. Flashes of his confrontation with The Man tore at his soul.

"I'll kill you." Bud had pressed the gun to The Man's temple, his own vision swimming from rage and whiskey. "I swear to God, I will make you eat these bullets one-by-one."

The Man was unmoved. He smiled, mouth closed, eyes bright as daggers. "Bud, Bud. You aren't going to kill me."

Bud dug the barrel in harder. "Oh, yeah? Watch me." Once he decided someone was going to die, they died.

So how had it all gone wrong...?

The Man's ugly smile only deepened, the grin of a soul that lived in an even lower circle of hell than Bud's own. The blood running down the side of his face only made him more sinister. "'Killing 'em all gets so boring.' Isn't that what you told me once? Didn't you tell me you were the cat that eats the legs off a spider, one-by-one? No, what you want is to torture me. Aren't I right?"

Bud cocked his head noncommittally. "Sure. I can torture you first. I'll leave you half a face if you like. You can have it for a whole hour. And then I'll kill you. No one puts a hit on me. You told Jimmy Beacon I killed his sister. You sicced him and his bomb on me."

"Jimmy who?" The folds of his smile diverted the trickle of blood. "I never heard of him."

"Why, you—" Bud grabbed a fistful of The Man's shirt.

"I'm not really the one you want to torture," The Man whispered. His eyes delved deep into Bud's, as if he were reading his soul like a book. "The person you want is beyond your reach. You can't get to him to give him what he truly deserves—because he's behind bars. The world is safe from him, and he is safe from you."

Bud backed away, lowering his gun, jaw slack.

But why had he lowered his gun? Why had he let The Man get to him?

Bud stared in disbelief. "You didn't..." was all he managed to say. He tilted his head, anger and injury mixing in a poisonous cocktail. "You had Skull investigate me?"

Lightning flashed, illuminating The Man's face. "Of course I did."

Bud crashed through thick bushes, the twigs and leaves scratching his bare arms. Where had he hidden his car? He couldn't even remember. He was lost in the woods around The Man's neighborhood, running frantically as if someone were chasing him. But no one was. No one but the ghosts of his past—and the voice of The Man ringing in his ears.

Bud had shaken his head in disbelief. Still, even if Skull had dug around in Bud's past, there was no way he knew all of it. Even back in the day, there was hardly a soul who had known the truth. There was no way The Man knew—

But as The Man went on, sickening dread filled his entire soul. Dread that he didn't have a secret in the world.

"The man you want is protected by too many people, by too many laws that were far too lenient for what he did to you. For what he did... to your lover."

Bud began to shake.

"Maybe you simply never found the nerve to fight your way through to the bastard who murdered Zayne Mars. Maybe then, you didn't know your own power. But ever since, you've taken out your fury on others. Innocent bystanders. After all, that's what you and Zayne were. Just innocent bystanders, living your lives together in a world that hated you for being different."

Bud backed away. His gun hand shook. He needed more control than this. He needed control...

The Man stared him down furiously, his keen eyes turning to rage, the blood dripping from his jaw. "You've lived nothing but murder and lies ever since. Do not threaten me for telling you the truth."

Bud fell head-long in the mud, the tears streaming down his face. He grabbed fistfuls of muck, leaves, and roots. They squeezed through his fingers, escaping his grasp just as any hope of happiness had.

"Zayne," he whispered to the night. Years ago, he had screamed it in the walls of his apartment, after seeing his boyfriend dead on the pavement. How could anyone hate so much? How could anyone hate something so beautiful as two human beings in love? What did it matter to anyone else?

"You want to torture the innocent?" The Man had asked, watching Bud's tears fall as if every one were precious to him. "Then do so. You have my blessing. I understand." And like a loving father, a pontificate who cared for his flock, he had welcomed Bud into his arms, let him lay his head on his shoulder, let him weep. "Believe me, I understand." His voice shuddered with emotion as he said it.

"Zayne," Bud whispered again. In all the years since Zayne's death, the name had barely passed his lips. The only way to move on had been to forget. And to let the pain escape any way it could find a way. Once he decided someone was going to die...

He bowed his head and wept. Zayne would never recognize the animal he had become. Everything that had once been beautiful was gone.

CHAPTER FORTY-FIVE
TOMMY

———— ✵ ————

Nancy tiptoed into the living room, tying a thick, fuzzy bathrobe. She crept to my chair and leaned over to whisper in my ear. "Is Wade outside?"

I nodded.

She folded her arms, as if warding off a chill, and huffed a sigh, staring at the door. She shuffled to a nearby ottoman and sat down, still holding herself tight, bouncing her foot. The job of being a cop's wife wasn't an easy one—never knowing just where your husband was, how much danger he was in, or if he'd even make it home that night. Nancy bore the stress with grace and poise. This was as visibly anxious as I'd ever seen her.

A cordless phone weighed down the pocket of her robe, as if she were ready to dial the station at a moment's notice. The thought flitted across my mind—hadn't Wade alerted the station already? Was he out there with no backup? Or was I just overthinking this? Had I only imagined a man outside the door?

Lightning flickered and thunder rolled in the distance. There were no voices. No commands to put hands in the air. No fleeing footsteps. Nothing.

Still, I envisioned what it would be like if the man who shot me was put behind bars tonight. And I suddenly realized how vast was the sea of mental energy he had claimed. Below the surface, I was drowning in fear and vigilance. Even here at Nancy and Wade's house—even with Wade actively searching the yard—it felt as if I were alone; as if there was no one else to take the watch.

I closed my eyes, clenching my teeth. There was nothing to worry about... There was nothing to worry about...

The door latch clicked. My eyes flew open. Wade stepped into the foyer, a splash of moonlight illuminating his shoulders and the back of his head. He secured the door behind him, then turned to look up at us. Even though his face was hidden in shadow, I thought I could read his disappointment.

He shook his head.

My heart crashed. The watch wasn't over...

"Nothing?" Nancy asked.

"Nothing." Wade climbed the steps, one hand on the railing, the other behind his back. I assumed he was keeping his gun out of sight again. "Just a squirrel trying to make a nest. It chewed a hole in the siding."

"A *squirrel?*" Nancy's voice actually squeaked in surprise.

Wade stepped into the living room and looked down at me. "Sorry it woke you."

I searched the shadows of his face. Did I believe him? Was he trying to withhold information from me again in a misguided effort to protect me from the facts?

Nancy reached over and flicked on a lamp. When she looked at her husband again, she shouted. "You're bleeding!" A trickle of blood ran from his temple to his chin. "Oh, look at your face."

"My face?" Wade lifted his hand to his head—and then we saw where the blood actually came from. It welled from

212

a cut in the skin between his first finger and thumb. He pulled his hand away and stared, as if seeing the cut for the first time.

Nancy rose and put a firm hand on her husband's chest. "Sit down. I'll get the first aid kit."

Wade caught her wrist with his bleeding hand and stopped her. Under his breath, he whispered, "I need a paper bag."

Nancy frowned. "A paper—?" Her eyes dropped to his other hand, which he'd taken from behind his back, but still concealed from me with his body and Nancy's. Her face illuminated. "Oh! Um... Here. I've got it."

I wasn't sure, but I thought she used a fold of her bathrobe to take something from Wade's hand. I strained to see. It looked like a piece of plastic cut from a disposable water bottle. I knew as well as Nancy why Wade wanted a paper bag—it was one of the best ways to store evidence without destroying delicate indicators like fingerprints. Still, I couldn't envision what was so vital about a square of plastic.

Wade sat down and elevated his injured hand, applying pressure. He seemed lost in his own thoughts. He looked pale. I couldn't imagine it was from blood loss; the cut really didn't look *that* bad.

"How'd you cut your hand?" I asked.

He took an extra second to respond. "Trying to flush out the squirrel. I must have cut it on the siding."

Why had he paused? To think up a lie? If I looked at that squirrel hole, would I find blood on the edge? Would I even find a squirrel hole? What was he trying to hide from me? Why did he insist on coddling me? What did a piece of plastic mean? I couldn't take this cloak and dagger anymore. I screwed up my nerve.

"You're lying."

Wade's eyes lifted. Met mine. His were dead inside. Exhausted. Angry.

213

I didn't care. "Wade. Quit acting like I'm made of glass."

He drew in a deep breath. "Fine. Okay. You're right. There was someone in the yard. I found a piece of plastic by the side door. It was dark, and I cut my hand on it."

"It's just a piece of trash," I said. "The storm could have blown it into the yard."

"You can also slip it into a door jamb to pop open a lock."

Lightning chose that moment to illuminate the room in eerie blue. Wade's gaze on me was unwavering.

"Does that make you feel better to know someone was trying to get in?" he asked.

The thought turned my stomach, so I opted not to dwell on it. Instead, I let my simmering temper build to a boil. "Being kept in the dark doesn't contribute to my sense of safety." Finding a soap box, I climbed right on up. "Wade, I'm aware someone shot me. I'm aware he's still out there somewhere." I waved vaguely toward the windows. "Let's quit pretending everything's fine. I need *more* information, not less."

Wade bowed his head and studied his hand. He let the blood soak into the cuff of his shirt, sacrificing that rather than Nancy's beige carpet. Part of me felt awful for chewing him out while he sat there bleeding.

At last he spoke. "I'm sorry. It's not always easy to know what to do." He tilted his head, as if studying a curiosity instead of his own hand. "Did you know that after I killed Bobby Markham, I had nightmares every night for three years?"

I had no words for that. I hadn't known. But his vulnerability, after all these years, deserved a response. I shook my head.

"You'd think I would have mentioned it. Maybe I thought talking about the nightmares would make them more real. Every night, I saw a kid I knew looking at me with absolute hatred in his eyes. And then he aims the gun

214

at me. And then I pull the trigger and kill the only son of a man I grew up with. That night never really ended. Just went on and on..."

At Wade's words, my own frustrations crept away, ashamed. I'd been so absorbed in my own feelings, I hadn't stopped to ponder *why* Wade might be handling me with kid gloves. There had been a time when the shoe had been on the other foot—when Wade had faced down a gun and someone reckless enough to use it on another human being.

"I became a cop so everyday people like you would never have to endure something that horrific. I signed up to serve and protect. And I failed." He looked at me. "I failed my best friend. I'm failing my entire town. People are dying. I lost one of my own men. And I can't stop it."

I sighed, and then I found that I had been turning the wedding band that Laina had given me. I forced my hands to be still. I guess I'd never been good at heart-to-hearts. Wade was far better at them than I had ever been. Somehow he'd managed to change my fury to guilt that I'd ever brought the topic up.

"You're doing fine, Wade," I managed to croak out while staring at a set of curtains. "Whatever madman's on the loose, you'll catch him. You always do."

Wade nodded his appreciation. "I'm sorry, Tommy. I'll try to be more open."

I just nodded. This conversation could be done now. I was sorry I'd brought it up.

Nancy swept into the room, arms laden with bandages and bottles of antiseptic. "Now, show me that hand." She settled onto the ottoman again, took her husband's hand and slapped a sterile pad over the cut. "It's barely bleeding now. Good. Oh, your poor shirt. That'll never come out. I can't believe all this over a squirrel—"

Wade stopped her in the middle of wrapping his hand with gauze. "I told him."

She blinked. "Oh." She looked for a moment like she was shifting gears. A second later, she had adjusted as if we'd been talking about a criminal the entire time and not a rodent. "Well, anyway, they never got in, whoever they were. The alarm would have gone off." She finished off Wade's bandage with tape. "Is that too tight?"

Wade flexed his fingers. "It's perfect."

"Should you call your detectives?" I asked.

Wade nodded and rose. "Guess I'll roust Lehman out of bed." He motioned with his bandaged hand. "Thank you, Nancy."

She smiled and nodded. Wade passed into his office, closing the door behind him. A moment later, we heard his muffled voice through the wall.

Nancy clasped her hands, as if to calm her own tremors. If I wondered whether I was still welcome company, she settled the question with her next words. "Well. How about a cup of tea? Once the cavalry gets here, it'll be impossible to get any sleep."

I nodded absently. I didn't want the tea. I wanted space to think. Nancy left, and I was grateful.

Roland's words swirled in my mind. *"Tommy, have you ever considered that Wade could be the fourth member of the ring?"*

No. And I never would. If Wade was behind the murders, why would his home be the target of a break-in?

The only scenario in which that made any sense was if the hunter was being hunted.

216

CHAPTER FORTY-SIX
SKULL

———————————⚓———————————

Skull slid behind the wheel of his car and stowed his gun in the glove compartment. He hadn't really needed it in the end. That was good. In fact, the entire mission had gone quite well. Clean. Efficient. His handiwork would never be noticed. Time to report to The Man.

He dialed, then turned the key in his ignition and calmly pulled out of the neighborhood. The phone rang four times. Had The Man already gone to bed?

At last, he picked up. "Yes?"

"I'm not waking you, am I?" Skull asked.

"No. It's been a busy night."

The abrupt way he said it—almost angrily—left Skull wondering what he meant. But in this line of business, you didn't ask unnecessary questions. So why did he feel... concerned?

The Man must have sensed it. That didn't surprise Skull. What did was the fact that The Man deigned to elaborate. "Bud was here. He tried to kill me."

Skull's grip convulsed on the wheel. "What—? Are you all right, sir?" What an idiot. Did Bud understand who he was messing with? He would wind up dead.

"I'm fine. Don't think of it. Give me your report. Is the job done?"

"Yes. The house is fully bugged, inside and out."

"The, ah—the devices. They'll never be found?"

"Never."

"Good. Good. Thank you."

Skull thought The Man sounded either distracted or vaguely incoherent. How bad had the encounter been? Was he hurt? Or just planning Bud's demise?

"I'll be in touch," said The Man. "I have another call to make. Good night."

"Good night, sir."

Skull let The Man hang up—it was good customer service—then dropped the hand with the phone into his lap.

The Plan felt off the tracks somehow. Did this change things? Then again, The Man was good at adjusting to the circumstances.

Skull had no idea what might happen next. He didn't imagine it meant anything good for Bud Weber.

CHAPTER FORTY-SEVEN
ROLAND

The phone line clicked alive. "Nine-one-one. What's your emergency?"

Emergency. Yes. The glass. The door exploding. He remembered that part clearly. And then he must have blacked out. He remembered coming to. And possibly blacking out again. What was left of his French door hung from one hinge, flopping in the wind.

"Yes, there was a break-in. I need an ambulance, please."

The handkerchief he pressed to his temple was no match for the blood streaming down his face.

"What's your address?"

"Nine Eighty South Lake Shore Drive."

"All right, sir, an ambulance is on the way."

The 911 operator went on to ask for more details—something about the nature of the break-in and his injuries. But the room was going topsy-turvy, and the woman's words made no sense. He tried to speak, but his voice failed him. In the end, he could latch onto only one thought.

Monica was going to kill him.

The room dimmed, then went black.

JOIN THE CREW

Ahoy, Shipmate!

If you feel like you're perched on a lighthouse, scanning the horizon for Danielle Lincoln Hanna's next book—good news! You can subscribe to her email newsletter and read a regular ship's log of her writing progress. Better yet, dive deep into the life of the author, hear the scuttlebutt from her personal adventures, spy on her writing process, and catch a rare glimpse of dangerous sea monsters—better known as her pets, Fergus the cat and Angel the German Shepherd.

It's like a message in a bottle washed ashore. All you have to do is open it...

DanielleLincolnHanna.com/newsletter

BOOKS BY DANIELLE LINCOLN HANNA

The Mailboat Suspense Series

The Girl on the Boat: A Prequel Novella
Mailboat I: The End of the Pier
Mailboat II: The Silver Helm
Mailboat III: The Captain's Tale
Mailboat IV: The Shift in the Wind
Mailboat V: *coming soon*

DanielleLincolnHanna.com/shopnow

ACKNOWLEDGMENTS

Twenty twenty was a terrible year for writing a book—at least for me. Unable to access my library and coffee shops, I was forced to write from home—something I already knew I was bad at. (That's why I *have* my library and coffee shops.)

So first and foremost, epic thanks to the two book coaches who saw me through, *Jacquelyn Scott* and *Tiffany Herron.* Thanks, ladies, for keeping my squirrel brain focused! Also, huge gratitude to *my patient fans,* who waited an extra year for this book to come out. Not only did you give me time and space to write, you continued to talk up my books while you were waiting, making this release the biggest one yet.

As always, my gratitude to the Lake Geneva Cruise Line (CruiseLakeGeneva.com), owners and operators of the real-life Mailboat. Special thanks to *General Managers Harold Friestad (ret.)* and *Jack Lothian,* to *the Mailboat Captain Neill Frame,* and to *Office Manager Ellen Burling.* Your combined contributions allowed my imagination to set sail.

I don't know why my characters decide to be what they are—I just know not to meddle with the process. So when Angelica Read informed me that she was Latina, I had my homework cut out for me. Prior to writing this book, I had had all of one conversation with someone of Mexican-American heritage (Sandra Cisneros' brother, ironically enough). Massive thanks to *Alondra Gaspar* for talking with me about her Mexican-American background, for reviewing my manuscripts, and for teaching me how to use both vulgarity and terms of endearment in Spanish. (At least on the page. My spoken Spanish will never sound as beautiful as hers.) Thanks also to our mutual friend *Michael O'Leary* for introducing us.

Much appreciation to *David Congdon,* Threat Assessment and Countermeasures Specialist. I always look forward to our conversations on my books from a psychological perspective.

Many thanks to my writer's club, *We Write Good,* and especially to *Elaine Montgomery* for telling me how good my manuscript was, and to *Rachel Surtshin* for telling me how bad it was. Seriously, Rachel, I appreciate your holding my feet to the fire. Thanks for questioning early attempts at Angelica's portrayal by speaking from your experiences with the Mexican-American community, and thanks for helping me clarify Monica's feelings by being a bad-ass feminist who couldn't understand anyone in Monica's circumstances regretting her choice. I wasn't satisfied until you were satisfied.

My thanks also to *Carrie Lynn Lewis,* my trusty brainstorming partner. Thanks for helping me find the path when I'm not sure where my characters have led me this time.

Before publication, this book was thoroughly examined by my sharp-eyed Early Reader Team. I promise, one day I'll know the difference between *suit* and *suite.* By name, thank you to *Susan Beatty, Stephanie Brancati, Kathy Collins, Brenda Dahlfors, Nancy Diestler, Lynda Fergus, Lisa McCann, Elaine Montgomery, Rebecca Paciorek, Linda Pautz, Pat Perkins, Sanda Putnam, JoAnn Schwartz Schutte, Kathy*

Skorstad, Suzette Titus, Judy Tucker, Lisa Vint, Kimberly Wade, Carol D. Westover, and *Mary-Jane Woodward.*

Also, a huge shout-out to the members of my very first Street Team, especially *Paula OBrien-Slaasted* for being the first to jump on board. Thanks, all of you, for helping me promote the new book and create a bigger splash than ever.

For their unique contributions that resulted in my stunning cover art, thanks to *Matt Mason Photography* (MattMasonPhotography.com) for the imagery, *W. J. Goes* for helping my photographers chase down the Mailboat, and *Maryna Zhukova* (MaryDes.eu) for bringing the images to life.

Rebecca Paciorek, Susan Beatty, and *JoAnn Schwartz Schutte,* you are the most enthusiastic, tireless, and determined group of publicists an author could ask for. I wouldn't be where I am without you. Looking forward to seeing you in Lake Geneva this summer!

More than my thanks—my heart and soul to those I hold close. *Fergus,* you've turned into such a cuddler, I'm not sure you're the same unhappy cat I adopted four years ago. *Angel,* that little German Shepherd puppy who couldn't sit still for a photo with the Lake Geneva PD is long gone— and you're actually growing into your name. And *Charles William Maclay.* Congrats on your graduation from Western Colorado University with a Master's of Fine Arts. Congrats on your first published short story. Congrats on placing in two separate screenwriting competitions. I'm so proud of you. Thanks for accomplishing all that while taking more than your fair share of duties so I could kick out another novel on time. Pretty soon, we won't be "the educated one" and "the successful one." We'll just be successful together.

Also, we survived a pandemic together without murdering each other. If that isn't winning at life, I don't know what is. I love you.

ABOUT THE AUTHOR

Danielle Lincoln Hanna is the author of the Mailboat Suspense Series. While she now lives in the Rocky Mountains of Montana, her first love is still the Great Plains of North Dakota where she was born. When she's not writing, you can find her hiking with her boyfriend Charles, adventuring with her German Shepherd Angel, and avoiding surprise attacks from her cat Fergus.

Made in the USA
Las Vegas, NV
27 September 2023

78211523R00142